LIBERTY PORTER,
First Daughter
Cleared for Takeoff

Don't miss any of Liberty Porter's awesome adventures!

ALSO BY JULIA DeVILLERS

LIBERTY PORTER, FIRST DAUGHTER

NEW GIRL IN TOWN

★ ★ ★ JULIA DeVILLERS ★ ★ ★
★ ILLUSTRATED BY PAIGE POOLER ★

LIBERTY PORTER,
First Daughter

Cleared for Takeoff

ALADDIN
NEW YORK   LONDON   TORONTO   SYDNEY

ALADDIN

An imprint of Simon & Schuster Children's Publishing Division

1230 Avenue of the Americas, New York, NY 10020

First Aladdin hardcover edition July 2011

Text copyright © 2011 by Julia DeVillers

Illustrations copyright © 2011 by Paige Pooler

All rights reserved, including the right of reproduction

in whole or in part in any form.

ALADDIN is a trademark of Simon & Schuster, Inc.,

and related logo is a registered trademark of Simon & Schuster, Inc.

For information about special discounts for bulk purchases,

please contact Simon & Schuster Special Sales at 1-866-506-1949 or business@simonandschuster.com.

The Simon & Schuster Speakers Bureau can bring authors to your live event.

For more information or to book an event contact the Simon & Schuster Speakers Bureau at 1-866-248-3049

or visit our website at www.simonspeakers.com.

Designed by Karin Paprocki

The text of this book was set in Bauer Bodoni.

The illustrations for this book were rendered digitally.

Manufactured in the United States of America 0611 FFG

2 4 6 8 10 9 7 5 3 1

Library of Congress Cataloging-in-Publication Data

DeVillers, Julia.

Cleared for takeoff / by Julia DeVillers ; illustrated by Paige Pooler. — 1st Aladdin hardcover ed.

p. cm. — (Liberty Porter, first daughter)

ISBN 978-1-4169-9130-4

I. Pooler, Paige, ill. II. Title.

PZ7.D4974Cl 2011

[Fic]—dc22

2010045056

ISBN 978-1-4424-2399-2 (eBook)

I wrote this book while living

in the country of Georgia while my husband

worked at the American Embassy.

Thus, for my new friends:

the people of Georgia.

LIBERTY PORTER,
First Daughter
Cleared for Takeoff

Chapter 1

IF YOUR FATHER HAS BEEN PRESIDENT OF THE United States of America for two whole months and you've been First Daughter *and* super-secret assistant to the president for the same amount of time, there are a few things you should know:

1. You get to go to cool places in your own neighborhood. Like museums that have dinosaurs, your mom's dress from Inauguration Day, and George Washington's false teeth.

2. You don't have to give your teeth to the museum, even if a bossy girl at school tries to make you think you do. (Whew!)

3. You have a great huge room to throw a party where even Chief of Staff Miss Crum will dance like a crazy person.

4. You don't get to have the White House staff clean up after your party. You have to clean up even the gajillion rainbow sprinkles that spilled.

5. Your Secret Service Agent will secretly help you sweep up the tricky sprinkles under the couch.

Liberty loved living in the White House. It was the house where every single president except for George Washington lived. A house where other First Kids had lived for more than two hundred years.

A house where more than one million tourists came through in a year! More than one million! Including kajillions of kids.

Liberty thought that would mean she would have kajillions of playdates. But that wasn't how it worked. She couldn't just walk down and invite people to come upstairs to her room and play.

She had tried that on her first day in the White House. She wasn't allowed to do that anymore. She had to make special plans for people to come over.

And she had no plans for today. That meant Liberty was lonely.

Liberty knew she was lucky she lived in the White

House. The White House had its own movie theater! Its own bowling alley! Its own playground!

But it would be nice to be able to share them with somebody today. Liberty had met some new friends at school, but today there was no school.

Liberty's teacher, Mr. Santo, had asked the class what they were going to do for the holiday weekend.

Some people were going to the ocean. Some were going to visit their grandparents. Someone was going camping. Everyone was going *somewhere*. Everyone except Liberty.

Then suddenly someone did come into her room. Franklin! Liberty's dog was back from his morning walk.

"Good boy," Liberty said, kneeling down to scritch Franklin behind the ears. "You came to play with me!"

Liberty picked up Franklin's favorite squeaky ball. She squeezed it in front of his nose and then tossed it.

Franklin looked at the ball. Then he yawned. Then he went over to his bed and circled it a few times. Then he plopped down on it and fell asleep.

"Wait, no," Liberty said. "Wake up and play! Look, your favorite tugging toy!"

Liberty waved his toy in front of his nose.

Franklin just lay there and snored.

Usually Franklin loved to play fetch. But apparently, all he wanted to do now was play dead.

"Franklin," Liberty tried again. "Wake up! You're not nocturnal like Roosevelt and Suzy."

Roosevelt and Suzy were her sugar gliders. They were only awake at night. So Liberty couldn't play with them now either.

Booooooooring. She needed ideas for something to do. Liberty looked at a poster on her wall. It was one of the posters her father used when he was running for president.

PORTER: A MAN WITH IDEAS FOR AMERICA!

Her father!

Maybe he would have ideas for his daughter.

Liberty took out her really cool turquoise cell phone.

She texted POTUS (DADDY).

That meant the president of the United States.

AM BORED. DO U HAVE IDEAS FOR ME?

Liberty waited. Then her cell phone *brrzp*ed back.

USE YOUR IMAGINATION.

That was the best he could do? Use her imagination?

Brrzp! Another text came in from him. Oh, maybe he

had another idea.

CLEAN UR ROOM.

Liberty should change that sign of his.

PORTER: A MAN WITH IDEAS FOR AMERICA!
BUT **BAD** IDEAS FOR HIS DAUGHTER.

Liberty texted back:

I'LL USE MY IMAGINATION. KTHXBAI.

Okay. Imagination time. Liberty decided she would pretend she was on vacation. She looked in her dresser drawers. She pulled out a T-shirt that said FUN IN THE SUN and bright yellow sunglasses shaped like suns. She also pulled a hula skirt over her jeans and put on a lei her father got her in Hawaii.

Now she looked like she was on vacation.

Liberty took her extra pair of sunglasses out and placed them on Franklin's nose. Franklin kept snoring.

"We're on a relaxing vacation," she said. "Well, you're definitely relaxed."

Liberty then put a bath towel on the floor and lay down on it. She closed her eyes and pretended she was on the beach.

Ah, she could feel the pretend sun. The pretend

sand. Then Liberty pretended she was in the ocean. She plugged her nose and flapped her arms around like she was swimming.

"Liberty, I—" Liberty's mom had stuck her head into the room. "May I ask why you are rolling around on the floor while wearing a hula skirt?"

Liberty stopped flapping and sat up.

"I am on vacation," she explained. "I was using my imagination. It was Daddy's idea."

"Oh," her mother said. "Well, I hope you're having fun."

"No, it's boring." Liberty sighed. "But you're here now, so can you play with me?"

"Sweetie, I'd love to, but I have to go to a meeting downstairs," her mother said.

"It's a vacation day for the country," Liberty complained. "For everyone except you and Daddy."

"Honey, you know that the president and the First

Lady have many commitments," her mother said. "You're welcome to come with me. I'm discussing the economic and political realities of—"

Erg. No and no.

"I'll just be downstairs until I have to leave, then," her mother said. "Let your agent know if you need anything."

That's who Liberty could play with: SAM! SAM was Liberty's special Secret Service agent. He was very tall and had no hair. His shiny bald head made it extra fun to pat him on the head during duck, duck, goose. Yes, SAM was excellent at playing games! Now the vacation fun could begin!

Liberty grabbed a walkie-talkie off her desk. Yes! Liberty had her own walkie-talkie to talk to her Secret Service agents. She had decorated the walkie-talkie with silver nail polish and pink and purple sequins.

"Hello, SAM?" Liberty said into the walkie-talkie.

Zzzzrblt! Sppkt! The walkie-talkie made static noises, and then a voice spoke.

"Ruffles, do you need me?"

Ruffles? SAM never called her by her official code name. Liberty had thought up a way better one: Rottweiler.

"Um, who is this please?" Liberty said.

"This is Russ," the walkie-talkie spoke.

Oh. Russ. He was another Secret Service agent. But he didn't play hide-and-seek. He wouldn't let Liberty play secret spies with the walkie-talkies, and he never wanted to play zombie tag.

"Is SAM there?" Liberty asked politely.

"SAM has the vacation day off. Do you need anything?" Russ asked.

Liberty told him no thanks, and then groaned. AUGH! SAM was on vacation! Liberty pictured SAM

lying on the beach. She wondered if he wore his dark secret agent suit and an earpiece in his ear on the beach.

Liberty had only one last hope. There was someone else who might be upstairs in the White House. It was Abraham Lincoln. Well, his ghost, anyway. Some people thought Lincoln's ghost still haunted the Lincoln bedroom. Maybe today would be the day she could get his ghost to talk to her.

Liberty went down the hall. The Lincoln bedroom

was super-fancy. This was where Lincoln signed the Emancipation Proclamation. There was a huge bed in it, and Liberty pulled herself up on it.

"Excuse me!" Liberty called out. "Mr. President Abraham Lincoln? Are you there?"

She waited.

"I know you're shy," she said. "But I'm really bored and lonely. Everyone is on vacation."

Liberty waited a minute. She was about to give up. And that was when she heard it.

"Hello?" a low voice said.

Liberty almost fell off the bed.

"President Abraham Lincoln?" Liberty asked. "Is that really you?"

"Yesss," the voice said. "Yessss, it issss."

Chapter 2

O H MY GOSH! OH MY GOSH! LIBERTY WAS talking to the ghost of Abraham Lincoln!

"Hi, Mr. President!" she said. "I'm Liberty! I live here now! But I sleep in a different bedroom. Yours is too spooky. No offense."

"Hello, Liberty," President Lincoln's ghost said.

"So this is really freaky," Liberty said. "Can I put you on hold for a minute? I want to get my parents. They'll never believe me."

"I can't stay long," President Lincoln's ghost said.

"I also can't hear you very well. Stand up on the bed and get closer."

She jumped on the bed and stood on her tiptoes.

"Can you hear me now?" she shouted at the ceiling.

"Yeeessss," President Lincoln's ghost said to her. "So you're bored because everyone is on vacation?"

"Yeah," Liberty nodded.

"I have been bored too. Maybe you can entertain me. Can you do the hula?"

Oh my gosh! Oh my gosh! President Lincoln could see her and wanted her to . . . what?

"Hula dance," he explained. "You're wearing a hula skirt and lei?"

"Oh, right." Liberty looked down at her outfit. She took a deep breath. Then she started to hula dance on the bed. She waved her hands in the air and jumped around the bed.

"I'm not the greatest dancer," Liberty apologized to President Lincoln's ghost.

"I can see that. I'm disappointed," President Lincoln's ghost said.

"Excuse me?" Liberty's jaw dropped.

"The first daughter should be a better dancer," he replied. "You're not Liberty Porter, First Daughter. You're Liberty Porter, Worst Dancer."

"Did you call me Liberty Porter, Worst Dancer?" Liberty gasped.

"Yes, I did, Piggerty Porter, First Snorter."

Wait a minute. Wait just one minute. There was only one person who called her Piggerty Porter, First Snorter. It was . . .

"Surprise!"

A boy burst through the door of the Lincoln bedroom. And yes, it was Max Mellon.

MAX MELLON! Max Mellon from her old home-town and her old school? Max Mellon who once told her she would probably sneeze green goo all over live television and he couldn't wait to see that?

Liberty's mouth dropped open in surprise.

"You look like you saw a ghost," Max said. "Oh wait, you just thought you were *talking* to a ghost. HA! I can't believe you fell for that."

Liberty sat down on the bed.

"What are you doing here, Max Mellon?" she asked.

Before Max could respond, their mothers entered the room.

"Hello, Liberty! It's lovely to see you," Max's mother said to her.

"Hello, Mrs. Mellon," Liberty said.

"We're flying out on vacation and our layover is here in Washington," Mrs. Mellon said. "I know my Maxie would love to spend more time with you, but we're happy we could sneak in an hour."

Whew! Liberty was worried he would be staying his whole vacation.

"Liberty, I'm sure you'll be a wonderful host and show Max around for a bit while I catch up with Mrs. Mellon," Liberty's mom said.

"Thank you, First Lady Mrs. Porter." Max smiled his best not-letting-grown-ups-see-how-evil-he-was smile.

The door closed. Max waited only one second.

"Liberty Porter Potty! Did you miss me?"

"No," Liberty told him.

"I wish I could have gotten a picture of you hula dancing like that," Max said, cracking up. "I could sell it to the magazines and make millions. Hula, hula!"

No more hula. Liberty took off her lei and slid off the hula skirt so she was in her normal T-shirt and jeans.

"Let's go!" Max said. "You have to tour me! Let's go see your room."

"Okay." Liberty sighed. They walked toward her room.

"I need to tell everyone what your room is like now," Max said. "Remember how your room used to be so messy? Now you have servants, though. So I guess your room is perfect. I can't make fun of that anymore."

Liberty stopped walking. She still had to clean her own room. That meant her room was messy. With a capital *M*. Liberty did not want Max to tell people that.

"You don't want to see my room. That's boring. You're in the White House," Liberty said. "You should see the *downstairs* part."

"Anyone can see that," Max complained. "I need the private-secret-behind-the-scenes places that only friends can see."

Liberty thought quickly.

"Max," she said. "*Downstairs* has a private choco-late shop."

Max stopped in his tracks.

"Chocolate shop?" he asked. "Like, eating *chocolate* chocolate shop?"

"Yes," Liberty said. "Yes and yes."

"Last one to the chocolate shop is a rotten egg," Max yelled.

He took off running down the hall. Liberty started after him but then stopped. She picked up her walkie-talkie and said something into it.

Chapter 3

L IBERTY, DID YOU REALLY THINK GOING to the chocolate shop in the morning was a good idea?" her father asked.

Liberty and her parents were in the living room. Max Mellon's family had to go, and they had all said good-bye. And then Liberty had to change her shirt, because of the chocolate pudding competition.

"It was a special occasion," Liberty said. "Max was visiting. Mom said I could visit the chocolate shop on special occasions. Max plus holiday equals special occasion?"

"That is true," her mother said. "But I believe you need permission first. There seem to be a lot of special occasions lately."

Oops.

"Liberty, do you think the chocolate pudding competition was a good idea?" her father asked her.

Oops again.

Max had double dared her to a chocolate pudding competition. It had all been his idea. Max hadn't been happy about being the last one to the chocolate shop. So he was the rotten egg.

"You had your Secret Service agent tell me the flower shop was the chocolate shop!" Max complained. "Of course you got there first. That's not fair."

Heh-heh. That was pretty genius. So they decided to have a fair and square eating contest. The cook had made éclairs with chocolate pudding in them. He gave them the leftover pudding.

"Whoever finishes first wins," Max had said. "But you can't use your hands."

Liberty had tried to slurp up her bowl of chocolate pudding as fast as she could. But she lost. And, she had gotten pudding all over her face and clothes.

And then Max had called her Needs-a-Bib-erty Porter.

"Sorry, Daddy," Liberty said to her father. "It wasn't a good idea. But Max wanted to see my room so he could tell my old class that it was messy."

"Hmm," her mother said.

"Then Max wanted to know why I was all alone. And he said I probably had no friends and everyone went on vacation to get away from me. And he called me Liberty Porter, First Loser.

"Hmm," her father said.

"I had to distract him!" Liberty wailed.

"The chocolate shop *is* a good distraction." Her father sighed.

"And," her mother said, "Max *is* a handful. I think cleaning up the mess you two made is enough of a consequence."

"Thank you, Mom," Liberty said. "I'm sorry."

"I'm sorry your vacation day hasn't been better," her father said. Then he looked at Liberty's mother. Liberty's mother looked at her father.

"Why are you looking at each other like that?" asked Liberty.

"Should we tell her the news?" her father asked her mother.

"Tell me! Tell me!" Liberty begged.

"We stayed home this weekend," her father said. "But next weekend we will be going away."

"Oh." Liberty stopped jumping. "You and Mom are going away?"

That wasn't good news. Who was going to stay home to watch her? Oh no. She hoped it wasn't Miss Crum.

Miss Crum was the chief of staff. Her job was to tell the president where he had to be and what he had to do. Miss Crum liked to tell Liberty what to do too.

Liberty shuddered.

"Liberty," her father said, "you're coming with us."

"I'm coming with you?" Liberty asked happily.

"Overseas," her mother added.

"Wait, I'm going to a different country?" Liberty started bouncing all over the place. NO WAY! She was going to a different country?

Liberty was very lucky. She had been all over America when her father was on his campaign. But she had never been to another country in her whole entire life.

"Yes." Her mom smiled.

Yessss! Liberty thought.

"Get your passporter, Liberty Porter!" her father said. "Ha, that was pretty clever. Get it? Passport-er?"

"I get it, Dad," Liberty said. That reminded Liberty of something Max Mellon would say.

HA! Liberty thought of something Max Mellon had said.

"I bet you're not going on vacation this weekend because your parents think you will embarrass them," said Max.

"That's not true," Liberty said. But then she thought about that. She hadn't been in the news since her first day of school. Liberty felt a little worried.

Liberty Porter was going to a different country! Take that, Max Mellon. Ha, ha, and HA!

"Did you know that the first president to go overseas was Theodore Roosevelt?" Liberty's dad asked her. "In 1906 he went to Central America to inspect the Panama Canal."

Liberty didn't know that.

"Up until then, there was a rule that presidents couldn't be more than three miles from America's shore," he said.

"Seriously?" Liberty asked. "They wouldn't let the president leave?"

"No, they thought it was too risky to be far from home," President Porter said. "Remember, there were no planes then."

"How did he get overseas?" Liberty asked.

"A ship," her dad answered. "However, we will be flying on Air Force One."

AIR FORCE ONE?! Liberty had never flown on Air Force One!

Air Force One was the official plane the president flew on.

Liberty wanted to have her own plane. It would be called Air Force LIBERTY!

She could imagine what her airplane would look like. Air Force Liberty would be turquoise, and the airplane wings would glitter and sparkle in the sun.

And inside, there would be furry pink carpets, and all the chairs would be super-squishy and soft.

She would have her own little cozy bedroom in it. It would be black and white and hot pink. And there would be a bed shaped like a cloud.

Air Force Liberty would have a Jacuzzi tub. A room for dance parties with a disco ball. A mini portable chocolate shop. Definitely a play place for Franklin and the sugar gliders, of course.

"So, Liberty, are you ready?" her father asked her.

"Do you solemnly swear to represent the children of America overseas?"

He held up his hand. Liberty held up her hand too.

It was their little joke. On Inauguration Day she thought he was making her take an oath of office. He really just wanted to high-five her.

"I solemnly swear to represent the children of America overseas by being awesome," Liberty said. And she would be awesome! She would be a secret assistant to the president: international version!

They were doing a high-five, low-five combination when someone else entered the room.

"Hello, Mr. President," Miss Crum said. "Mrs. Porter, Ruffles."

Miss Crum always called her by her secret code name, Ruffles.

"We were just telling Liberty about our exciting trip overseas," her mother said to Miss Crum.

"That *is* exciting," Miss Crum said. "And a big responsibility, too."

"I know." Liberty grinned. "I'm going to do my best to represent the children of America when I'm overseas. I just took an oath."

"I'm glad you appreciate that." Miss Crum nodded approvingly.

"I do!" Liberty said. "And I get to go in Air Force One for the first time!"

"Did you know that Franklin D. Roosevelt was the first president to fly in an airplane while in office?" Miss Crum asked them.

"Isn't that interesting?" her father said to Liberty.

That *was* interesting.

"The first plane that was the president's plane was called the Sacred Cow," Miss Crum said.

Ha! That was a silly name.

"Imagine flying on a plane named Sacred Cow." Miss Crum laughed. Liberty laughed too.

Sometimes Miss Crum wasn't so bad. Then she reached over and patted Liberty's hair.

"Liberty, you have something sticky in your hair," Miss Crum said, not approvingly. "Is that *chocolate?*"

"Erm." Liberty wriggled away.

"Chocolate in your hair?" said Miss Crum. "How on earth do you have all that chocolate in your hair?"

"Uh . . ." Liberty couldn't think of how to explain that. "I was eating chocolate pudding without using my hands."

"Oh dear, pudding should be eaten with your hands. And a spoon," Miss Crum said.

"I know, but—," Liberty tried to speak.

"Perhaps Liberty needs to brush up on her manners. This gives me a fabulous idea," Miss Crum said. "There's a class Liberty can take before she goes overseas."

Uh-oh.

"What kind of class?" her mother asked.

"It's for young diplomats," Miss Crum said. "A diplomat is a person who represents her country in another country."

That sounded okay. Maybe it wasn't such a bad idea after all.

"It is taught by James's mother," Miss Crum continued.

Or maybe it was a bad idea. James's mother was chief of protocol. Protocol meant MANNERS. And she was very, very serious about manners. Liberty groaned just thinking about it.

"It will help refresh Liberty on her manners before the trip!" she said.

Liberty let out a groan.

"Groaning at an adult is not nice manners," Liberty's father said, looking at Liberty. "Miss Crum is giving us helpful ideas."

Liberty groaned again. But this time, inside her head only.

"Let's sign Liberty up for that," her mother said.

"Excellent. Now, Mr. President and Mrs. Porter, I came to let you know it's time for your lunch meeting," Miss Crum said.

"Wait!" Liberty shouted. "Wait!"

The grown-ups turned around.

They couldn't leave yet! They still hadn't told her one major important thing: WHERE WAS SHE GOING?

"What country are we going to?" Liberty asked them.

"Sorry," her father said. "We can't tell you that yet. We'll surprise you."

"Surprise me?" Liberty said.

"Security purposes," Miss Crum explained. "We can't have any leaks."

"I don't leak!" Liberty said. "I can keep a secret!"

She could! Well, except for the time she told her mother what her father had gotten as a birthday present. Oh, and that time she slipped about her father's surprise party . . .

Liberty sighed.

"You're right. Surprise me," she agreed.

Chapter 4

VACATION WAS OVER AND LIBERTY WAS BACK to school.

SAM was line leader today. Well, actually Kayden was line leader, but she liked to give her turn to SAM. SAM carried the basket with all the lunch boxes in it.

The class was going to the cafeteria for lunch.

"SAM, what did you do on your vacation?" Kayden asked SAM.

"I went fishing and read a good book," SAM said.

"I can tell you were in the sun." Kayden nodded. "Your head is red and shiny."

SAM patted his bald, sunburned head and smiled.

Liberty sat at a lunch table between her new friends Preeta and Quinn. Quinn's twin brother Cheese Fries sat across from them.

"I went to a hotel with a huge pool," Cheese Fries said. His real name was Jack, but Liberty called him Cheese Fries. "I knocked my sister in with her clothes on. Heh."

"That was *not* my favorite part," his sister said.

"I bet Liberty went someplace really exciting," said Preeta, who sat next to her.

"Nope," Liberty said. "I was in my house the whole time."

"*Boooooring*," Cheese Fries said.

"Sometimes," Liberty agreed. "A boy from my old school visited me. He reminds me a lot of Cheese Fries."

"He must be awesome," Cheese Fries said cheerfully, as he opened a thermos.

Liberty decided to change the subject.

"I did find out I'm going on vacation soon, though," she said. "I'm going to another country!"

"You're going overseas?" Preeta asked. "That's so exciting."

"Yup and yup," Liberty agreed. "Liberty Porter, world traveler."

"You'll love it," Quinn said. "But wait. Where are you going?"

"Um, not sure yet," Liberty said.

"Umnotshuryet? Where's that?" Cheese Fries asked her.

"I'm not sure yet. They won't tell me until right before we leave." Liberty sighed.

"They probably have to keep it secret for presidential security." Preeta nodded.

"Yeah, you might go blabbing all about it," Cheese Fries said. "Blabberty Porter. Hah!"

Yes, Cheese Fries reminded her a lot of Max Mellon. Way too much.

"Do you know how to speak other languages? Maybe you'll have to learn a new language," Preeta said.

"In a week?" Uh-oh. Liberty didn't think she could learn a new language in a week.

"We better start," Preeta said. "I know how to say hi in Spanish: *hola.*"

"And *salut,*" Quinn added.

"*Namaste,*" said Preeta.

"And *privyet,*" Cheese Fries said. "That's Russian. *Kumusta ka, Assalamu alaikum, ni hao, shalom, ya soo, halo, ciao, ohayou gozaimas, moien, selamat datang, hei, oi, tja, salam.* Oh, and *bok.*"

Everyone was looking at Cheese Fries like . . . HUH?

"Wow," Liberty said.

"I like languages." Cheese Fries shrugged, taking a bite out of his apple.

"You would sound friendly anywhere in the world." Preeta looked impressed.

"So, Liberty, where in the world are you hoping to go?" Quinn asked her. "Maybe you're going to Paris to see the Eiffel Tower."

Liberty imagined herself in Paris, eating a yummy pastry by the Eiffel Tower.

"Or Australia to see koala bears!" Preeta said.

Ooh! Liberty would love to see koala bears close up.

And Australia is where sugar gliders are! She could visit Roosevelt and Suzy's cousins!

"Or to Egypt to see the pyramids," said Preeta. "Or London to see the Queen!"

Liberty pictured herself visiting the Queen. She would have to learn how to curtsy, but that would be worth it to meet the Queen. Maybe she would let Liberty wear her crown!

"Or maybe you're going to one of those countries where they eat tarantulas," Cheese Fries said.

Liberty did *not* want to imagine that. She shuddered.

"That could be what you're going to have to do." Cheese Fries shrugged. "They'll feed you squirmy spider legs. . . ."

Cheese Fries slurped up some chicken noodle soup from his thermos. He let some noodles hang out of his mouth like a spider. Then he slurped them up.

Slllurp!

"Ewwww," Liberty said.

"That is disgusting," his sister said. "Do you have any manners at all?"

"Too bad he can't go to manners class with me," Liberty said.

"Manners class?"

"Yeah, it's run by—" Liberty looked up and saw James sitting at a table with his class. "James! Hey, James!"

James wiped his mouth with his napkin and came over. Everyone said hi to him.

"Did you hear I have to take your mother's class?" Liberty asked him.

"She told me. That's really fun," James said.

"Fun for you, maybe," Liberty grumbled. "A manners class?"

"I thought it was the junior diplomats class," James said.

"It is, but isn't that a fancy name for manners?" Liberty asked him.

"It's very useful," James insisted.

"Pffft, manners," Cheese Fries said, with his mouth full. He sprayed french fry pieces all over the table.

"Ewwww!" everyone yelled. Liberty jumped up to avoid the spray and—*splat!*—knocked over Preeta's grape juice.

"Sorry!" Liberty yelled.

"Ack!" everyone else yelled. They jumped off their chairs and backed away from the purple spreading all over their table.

"Cleanup at table four!" one of the cafeteria aides yelled.

Mr. Santo was on cafeteria duty that day. He came running over with paper towels.

"Sorry!" Liberty said. "I knocked over the juice."

Cheese Fries looked guilty.

"It was my fault," he said. "I splatted out fries."

"See, you totally need a manners class," Quinn grumbled, as she helped wipe the table.

"I have to go to a manners class," Liberty told her teacher. "I wish everyone could do it with me."

"Manners are certainly a useful thing to learn," Mr. Santo agreed. He walked away to throw the soggy paper towels in the trash.

That gave Liberty an idea.

"What if we could have manners class at school?" she asked.

"Glak, no!" Cheese Fries said.

"It's pretty fun," James interrupted. "My mother brings really good food to eat to practice table manners. And excellent desserts."

"Hm," Cheese Fries said. "Would we miss classes? Then I'm in!"

"Be right back," Liberty said to everyone. She ran

to the side of the cafeteria where SAM was standing.

"SAM, I have an excellent idea. Would you please call Miss Crum and ask her if my whole class can take the junior diplomats class?"

"After school," SAM said.

"Pretty please?" Liberty said. "When have I ever asked to talk to Miss Crum if I didn't have to?"

"True," SAM said.

He pulled out his cell phone and dialed Miss Crum.

"Hello, Ruffles?" Miss Crum answered. "Aren't you in school?"

"Yes, but I have an important educational idea," Liberty said. "My whole class should take the junior diplomats class!"

"The whole class?" Miss Crum said. "I was thinking more of one-on-one training for you with James's mother. Then you have personal attention."

"Well." Liberty paused. "There are people in my

class whose manners need some help. Like, this one boy who sits next to me in class chews with his mouth open. I think I'm picking up his bad habit."

Liberty started making smacking noises with her lips.

"Oh dear," Miss Crum said.

"And this girl who always yawns when other people are talking. I think it's rubbing off on me."

"Well, that's just rude—," Miss Crum started to say, when Liberty interrupted her by letting out a big *yaaaawwwwn*.

"Oh dear!" Miss Crum said. "Perhaps something can be arranged."

Liberty skipped back to her lunch table.

"Who wants to go to manners class?" she asked.

Chapter 5

"WELCOME, JUNIOR DIPLOMATS."
James's mother was waiting at the
classroom door.

Yup, Mr. Santo's fourth-grade class had turned into
the junior diplomats class!

Liberty was already at her seat. She usually got to
class first, because she had to come in a special car.
That car was followed by a couple of other cars. It was
a little like a parade.

"Good morning, ma'am," Emerson said as she came
in, and smiled at Mrs. Piffle.

"What a polite young lady." Mrs. Piffle smiled back.

Kayden and Harlow imitated Emerson as they came in behind her.

"'Sup," Cheese Fries said, walking in. He held up his fingers in a peace sign.

"Oh my," Mrs. Piffle said. "I see we have our work cut out for us with others."

"Sorry about my brother," Quinn said as she entered behind him. "Hello."

"Good morning, junior diplomats. I'm Mrs. Piffle," Mrs. Piffle said. She wrote her name in fancy cursive on the whiteboard.

"This better be good," Cheese Fries whispered to Liberty.

"Who knows what a diplomat is?" Mrs. Piffle asked the class.

"An official who represents a country in another country," Emerson answered.

"Yes," Mrs. Piffle said. "When you're overseas, you want to represent not only yourself but your country."

Everyone nodded.

"First impressions are important. Let us learn the proper way to greet others," Mrs. Piffle said. "Would someone like to help me demonstrate?"

Emerson's hand shot up. She stood up and went to the front of the room. She did a perfect curtsy to Mrs. Piffle and then to the class.

"That was lovely," Mrs. Piffle said. "Curtsying is appropriate at some formal times. I was thinking of starting with a handshake."

"Oh," Emerson said, sitting down.

Mrs. Piffle put everyone in pairs. Liberty's partner was Kayden.

"A handshake is a greeting and shows confidence. The first step is to introduce yourself," Mrs. Piffle said.

"Hello, I'm Liberty," Liberty said.

"Hello, I'm Kayden," Kayden responded.

"Yo, dude," Jack said to his partner, Adam.

Mrs. Piffle squinted at Jack.

"I feel stupid introducing myself to Adam," Jack complained. "He knows me."

"Then let's switch partners," Mrs. Piffle said. "You can be mine."

Liberty tried not to crack up as Jack had to go and be Mrs. Piffle's partner. She could hear Jack groan as he went over.

"Class, eyes up here, please," Mrs. Piffle said. "Let's think about what first impressions we make. Jack, let's pretend you're the ambassador to Japan."

"Cool," Jack said.

Mrs. Piffle suddenly dropped her shoulders and slouched. She held up her hands in sideways peace signs and nodded.

"Yo, yo, homeslice," she said in a deeper voice. "Wassup?"

Liberty's jaw dropped. She wasn't expecting that from Mrs. Piffle! The whole class started to laugh.

"Now, is that the impression we should make as young diplomats?" Mrs. Piffle straightened up as her usual self.

"No," the whole class chanted.

"That was pretty cool, though," Jack said to her admiringly. Liberty had to give Mrs. Piffle one cool point for her imitation.

Mrs. Piffle taught them how to introduce themselves. Then she taught them how to shake hands.

Mrs. Piffle came over to them to test them out.

"Hello, I'm Liberty Porter." Liberty smiled at Mrs. Piffle and shook her hand.

"Class!" Mrs. Piffle suddenly called out. "Eyes up

here, please. Liberty is shaking hands too limply. This is called a limp fish handshake."

Everyone giggled at her. Oh, great.

"You'll want to use a firm handshake." Mrs. Piffle gripped Liberty's hand harder. "But you also don't want to arm wrestle."

Mrs. Piffle paused and walked over to Cheese Fries and Adam, who were arm wrestling like crazy.

"I win!" said Cheese Fries. Then he noticed Mrs. Piffle standing above him.

"Handshakes are not contests." Mrs. Piffle sighed. "I think it would be a good time for a lunch break."

"Woo-hoo, let's eat!" Cheese Fries shouted.

"Let's work on dining etiquette first," Mrs. Piffle told him.

Suddenly some people in black-and-white tuxedos entered the class. They were carrying silver trays.

"Ooh, fancy!" Kayden exclaimed.

The fancy servers passed out plates, a bunch of forks, spoons, napkins, and glasses.

Mrs. Piffle taught them how to set the table. She taught them how to hold a glass, which fork was used for which food, and how to wipe their mouths with napkins.

"Pay attention," Quinn had whispered to her brother on that one.

"I can't," he groaned. "This is making me hungry."

"Good timing," Mrs. Piffle said. The servers started bringing out food.

Yeesss! Food!

"Our first course will be soup," Mrs. Piffle said. "Please place your napkins on your laps and wait until everyone is served."

Cheese Fries put his spoon back down.

"And now we'll practice our lessons," Mrs. Piffle said. "By remembering what *not* to do."

"What *not* to do?" Emerson asked.

"We will play a guessing game. Each of you will demonstrate the opposite of manners," Mrs. Piffle said. "I'll give an example."

Mrs. Piffle picked up her soup and then

Sluuuuuuurp!

"You aren't supposed to slurp your soup loudly!" Emerson called out.

"Right," Mrs. Piffle said. "I'll demonstrate one more."

Buuuuuurp!

"Did Mrs. Piffle just burp?" Liberty looked at Mrs. Piffle in surprise.

"You aren't supposed to burp!" everyone yelled.

"Very good," Mrs. Piffle said, daintily wiping her mouth with her napkin.

"I can't believe Mrs. Piffle slurped and burped!" Liberty laughed.

"Awesome!" Cheese Fries said. "I want to try!"

"You must think of your own idea," Mrs. Piffle said.

"I've got one!" Harlow said. She leaned on the table and ate some soup.

"No elbows on the table!" Emerson called out.

They all finished their soup, slurping and burping. Then the next server brought out chicken, noodles, and carrots.

"Ew, this chicken looks gross," Cheese Fries said.

"Jack has contributed his example of bad manners," Mrs. Piffle said. "Who wants to go next?"

"Wait!" Cheese Fries said. "That wasn't my example! I was just saying—"

"Insulting the food is poor manners," Mrs. Piffle said. "Next."

Quinn reached across the table, knocking over an empty cup.

"Don't reach across the table!" everyone shouted.

Emerson had her turn: She forgot to say please. Kayden surprised everyone with excellently loud chewing with her mouth open.

"Ew, gross!" everyone said. Kayden looked pleased with herself.

Cheese Fries waved his hand in the air.

"Yes, Jack. You may have a turn," Mrs. Piffle answered.

"Mffffbrrrtttp. Bfffpkus!" Cheese Fries said, with his mouth stuffed full of food.

"Don't talk with your mouth full!" everyone shouted, then yelled, *"Ewwww!"* as noodles flew out of his mouth.

Cheese Fries grinned at his success.

Liberty tried to think of something good. Everyone was thinking of the same ones she was. She was the only person left to think of something. It was her turn. What could she do to be funny too?

"Liberty, your turn." Mrs. Piffle put her on the spot.

Um! Um! Liberty felt pressured to perform.

Just then the server brought out dessert. It was chocolate ice cream. Liberty thought back to her day with Max Mellon. She put her face down to her ice cream bowl and started eating the ice cream with no hands.

"Use a spoon!" everyone shouted. Everyone started cracking up when Liberty raised her face from the bowl.

"Ew, you're all chocolaty," Harlow said, frowning.

Liberty could feel chocolate dribble down her face.

"Well, that was an enthusiastic example, Liberty," Mrs. Piffle said. "Perhaps too enthusiastic. Why don't you go clean yourself off?"

SAM stepped inside the door to walk her down the hall.

"Wait!" Kayden said. "What about SAM's example of bad manners?"

"Bad manners?" SAM said. "I could start a food fight."

Everyone yelled, "Yeah!"

"Food fight!" Sydney yelled out, lifting a piece of bread.

"Wait! No! I was kidding," SAM called over the noise.

"Good heavens! No food fight, SAM," Mrs. Piffle said. "Children! Settle down! Settle down!"

"We better get out of here," SAM muttered to Liberty.

Hee! SAM and Liberty made their escape.

"I was only joking," SAM said. "Whew, that got crazy."

"You can't joke about food fights," Liberty said seriously. But she thought of SAM's face when Sydney believed him. Hee hee!

Liberty went into the girls' room and looked in the mirror. Her face was covered in chocolate. She washed a bit out of her hair. She hoped Miss Crum wasn't going to see her again.

"Sorry," Liberty said to Mrs. Piffle as she went back into her class.

"I hadn't thought of that one," Mrs. Piffle said to her. "Nor the food fight idea. Next time I'll be more specific."

Liberty stayed clean through the rest of the manners class. Mrs. Piffle taught them how manners were very different in some countries.

In some countries, a nod means no and shaking your head means yes. That could be confusing. In some places, burping after you eat is a compliment. And Liberty's favorite: In some places, sticking out your tongue is a friendly greeting!

When they had all stuck out their tongues at one another—including Mrs. Piffle—Mrs. Piffle asked if they had any questions.

"May we learn to curtsy, please?" Kayden asked.

"I'm not sure you'll need to curtsy," Mrs. Piffle said.

"I definitely won't!" Cheese Fries said.

"Please?" Kayden asked. "What if Liberty is going to meet the Queen and she needs to curtsy?"

Ooh! What *if* Liberty was going to meet the Queen? Liberty imagined herself in a fancy dress entering a beautiful palace.

There would be unsmiling guards in a line. One would announce:

"Presenting Liberty Porter, First Daughter of the United States of America!"

Liberty would walk through the line of guards. Then she would do a perfect curtsy. The crowd would ooh and aah.

In real life, Liberty turned out to be pretty terrible at curtsying. Kayden could practically touch her nose to the floor. Liberty fell over almost immediately.

"Hope there's no Queen to curtsy to wherever you're going, Liberty," Cheese Fries said cheerfully.

"Thanks," Liberty muttered, toppling over again. She was starting to think that too.

"Aren't you just dying of suspense to know where you're going?" Emerson asked her.

Liberty was!

"Wherever Liberty is going, the most important thing to remember when you go to a different country is to be very respectful of their people and culture," Mrs. Piffle said.

That was true. However, Liberty was still dying to know what culture and people she would be respecting.

Then she wondered if there were any countries where food fights *were* good manners. That would be an excellent place to go.

Chapter 6

NO PEEKING," HER MOTHER CALLED OUT from Liberty's bedroom.

Rats. Liberty sat down in the hallway and waited.

She had been trying to peek into her room as her mother was putting piles of her clothes into a suitcase. A winter coat would mean Liberty was going somewhere cold, like Iceland! Or Antarctica!

Or were there shorts and bathing suits for somewhere warm? Like Africa! Or Thailand!

It was dizzying to think about.

"Pssst, Franklin," Liberty whispered. Franklin trotted over to her.

"Fetch," Liberty whispered. "Fetch something my mom is packing from my suitcase so I can see it."

Franklin trotted into Liberty's room. Two seconds later he trotted out, carrying his squeaky ball.

"That's not helpful," Liberty said. But she patted him on the head and tossed his squeaky ball.

Liberty's mom came out of her room, rolling the suitcase.

"We're leaving soon," Liberty complained. "When do I find out?!"

She didn't get an answer, because her dad walked in.

"Liberty, are you ready?" her father, the president of the United States, asked.

Oh yes! Liberty was ready.

"Liberty Porter, we're going off to the air-porter!" her father said. "We're the air-Porters! Get it?"

"I got it." Liberty laughed. "Now, where are the air-Porters going?!"

Augh. No answer. Liberty spent the whole car ride to the airfield trying to trick everyone into telling her where they were going.

"Please tell me now where I'm going," Liberty asked her mother.

"Not yet," her mother answered.

"How about now?" She aimed that one at her dad.

"Nope," he answered.

"Psst, SAM! Where am I going?" Liberty whispered to SAM.

"Classified," SAM said.

Grrr.

When they got out of the car, Liberty could see a huge airplane.

And Liberty meant HUGE! Liberty's mom told her it was as tall as a six-story building and as long as a hockey field. It was white and turquoise blue, Liberty's favorite color! It said UNITED STATES OF AMERICA. The presidential seal was on its front. And on its tail, the American flag.

So patriotical!

The door to Air Force One opened.

Some men and women in military uniforms came down the steps. Then they stopped and saluted the president. Liberty's father saluted them back.

President Porter shook hands and said hello to the crew and boarded the airplane first. Her father knew the pilot, because every new president gets a new pilot who will fly them around.

Then it was Liberty's turn to board. She stopped and saluted everybody too.

A woman in a pilot uniform smiled and held her

hand out for Liberty to shake. Liberty remembered her best non-limp-fish-handshake manners and shook the pilot's hand strong.

"Welcome, Liberty Porter!" the pilot said. "What a nice handshake. I'm your pilot, Captain Tanya Stone. I hear this is your first trip on Air Force One."

"It is!" Liberty said, bouncing around. "It's even my first time going to a different country!"

"Liberty, it's an honor to have you and your family aboard." The captain smiled. "Come on in."

Liberty followed her up the steps and into AIR FORCE ONE!!!!

She looked to the left. She had a quick peek at what looked like an office with a desk and chair.

"You fly the plane out of an office?" Liberty asked.

"No, the flight deck is actually upstairs." Captain Stone smiled again.

"There's an upstairs?" Liberty asked. "It's a double-decker airplane!"

"I need to go up to the deck," the pilot told her. "Let's get this trip started!"

"Let's go find a seat for takeoff," Liberty's mom told her. "Your dad is going to have a meeting in a different part of the plane. I thought we'd start out here."

She showed Liberty to a row with a couple of comfy-looking seats. On one of the seats was her beanie dog that looked like Franklin!

"Yay." Liberty picked up the beanie dog and put it in the empty seat next to her.

"You may want to keep that seat free," her mother said.

"For SAM?" Liberty asked.

"For a surprise," her mother answered.

"Is the surprise you're going to tell me where we're going?" Liberty asked.

"This is an extra surprise," her mother told her.

"So many surprises." Liberty sighed dramatically.

"Close your eyes," her mother said. "No peeking."

Liberty heard a little bit of commotion, but she kept her eyes closed and petted her beanie dog. La la la. La dee do . . .

"Open your eyes," a different voice said. Wait, she knew that voice. It was

JAMES!

"No way!" Liberty said. "Are you coming with us to the mystery country?"

"Yep," James said. "My mother finally agreed. She said it would be an educational experience for me."

"And you'd make sure I used my manners, right?"

James grinned, and Liberty knew she'd guessed right. Mrs. Piffle thought James was a good influence on Liberty. He pretty much was.

"My mom is here too," James said. "She has to make

sure your *dad* uses good manners. Now, buckle up."

Liberty buckled up with the seat belt that had the presidential seal on it. She felt like such a jet-setter.

"This is so awesome," she said. "We're going to have so much fun in . . . Wait! We don't even know where we're going!"

James looked guilty.

"You know where we're going, don't you?" Liberty shouted. "Argh! Does everybody on this plane know where we're going except for me?"

"Well, I know the pilot does," James said.

Liberty leaned out of her seat into the aisle.

"I can't take it anymore! I'm about to burst out of the seat belt!" she cried. "There will be little tiny pieces of exploded Liberty Porter all over Air Force One if you don't tell me where we are going!"

"Looks like I'm just in time." Liberty's father said, walking down the aisle.

He cleared his throat for the big announcement.

"Liberty Porter, First Daughter," he said, "you are going to . . ."

Liberty was holding her breath.

". . . Georgia!"

"Georgia?" she cried. "I've *been* to Georgia. We campaigned in Georgia, and Florida, and South Carolina. That's not out of the country."

"Liberty, we're going to a different Georgia," he said. "THE COUNTRY OF GEORGIA."

Oh!

"Georgia is a country near Turkey and Russia," James said, pulling out his GPS. Liberty looked and could see a small country with a sea on one side, and yep, it was just under Russia.

"Some people think it's in Europe, and other people think it's Asia," James continued.

"Oh, that's cool," said Liberty, "then it's like I'm visiting two continents in one."

"Are you surprised?" her father asked.

Liberty nodded. She was definitely surprised. She had at least thought she would be going to a country she knew about.

"I think you'll like it there, Liberty," her father said, and smiled. "I've been told the Georgian people are very welcoming and friendly. This will be my first time in Georgia too. I thought it would be special for us to visit a place for the first time together."

"Then . . . cool!" Liberty said. "How do you say 'cool' in Georgian?"

"We'll ask the interpreter," Liberty's father said. "Enjoy your takeoff. I need to head to the front for a meeting."

He kissed her on the head and high-fived James.

The pilot's voice came over the loudspeaker. "Prepare for takeoff. Welcome to Air Force One. Destination: Georgia."

SAM walked up and down the aisle muttering into his walkie-talkie. *Brbzzzbrzrmrbzrrr.*

The plane started to taxi down the runway. Faster, faster, then Liberty felt her seat tilt and they were off, flying into the sky. She looked out the window and watched as they flew over the Potomac River below. Then they circled over the city of Washington, D.C.

"Look, it's the Washington Monument," James pointed.

Liberty could see the tall, pointy monument out the window. It looked really close.

"Look, there's the Lincoln Memorial," Liberty said, "and the Smithsonians."

Liberty had gone to the Smithsonian Museums for a field trip with her class. From the ground they looked huge, but up here in the sky, they got tiny. Liberty could see teeny little people like ants walking around the National Mall.

"And look, Liberty, there's your house," James exclaimed.

There was the White House!

"Bye, home! Bye, Franklin!" Liberty waved out

the window. "I wish Franklin could come."

James nodded. He was "sensitive" to dogs. That meant he was afraid of them. But he had gotten used to Franklin. Sometimes he even patted Franklin on the head.

"Bye, sugar gliders!" Liberty continued. "Bye, Abraham Lincoln's ghost—but not Max Mellon's fake Abraham Lincoln's ghost! Bye, movie theater. Bye, bowling alley. And good-bye, chocolate shop."

Liberty watched as the White House got smaller and smaller and then, as they flew into a cloud, she couldn't see her home anymore.

Chapter 7

LIBERTY WATCHED THE BIG, PUFFY WHITE clouds out her window.

"I feel like I'm in cotton candy," she said. Mmm, cotton candy. That made her think of something.

"Is there dessert on this plane?" she turned around and asked her mom.

"Yes," her mother said, "after lunch."

Just at that moment, a man walked up and handed Liberty a menu. His tag said: CFA.

"Hello, I'm Chief Flight Attendant Bruce. It's my

pleasure to offer you lunch today," he said. "A special menu just for you two."

"Thanks," Liberty said, and she and James checked out the menu.

Air Force One
Presidential Kids Menu

TURKEY SANDWICH IN THE SKY

CORN DOG IN THE CLOUDS

FLYING FRIES

THE PILOT'S FAVORITE GRILLED CHEESE

SOARING CHEESE AND FRUIT PLATE

DESSERT OF THE DAY

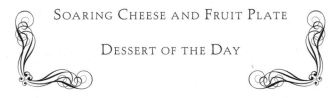

"The pilot likes grilled cheese?" Liberty asked.

"Loves it," CFA Bruce said.

"I'll definitely have that," Liberty said. "With a soaring fruit plate and of course, dessert."

"And to drink?"

"Do you have lemonade?" Liberty asked.

"Regular or pink?"

"Ooh, pink," Liberty said happily. James ordered Corn Dog in the Clouds, Flying Fries, and regular lemonade.

"I'll bring it out to you in a bit," CFA Bruce said, writing their order down.

"Now what do we do?" Liberty asked James. He shrugged. Liberty turned around to ask her parents what they could do, but her parents were gone.

"Your parents have gone up to the presidential suite," CFA Bruce told her. "Do you want me to get them for you?"

"Can we walk around?" Liberty asked.

"Of course," he answered. "Would you like a tour of the plane?"

"Yes!" Liberty and James both practically shouted.

They unfastened their seat belts and got up to follow CFA Bruce toward the back of the plane. They walked down a small hallway.

"On your left is the conference and dining room," CFA Bruce told them.

Liberty saw a large dining room table surrounded by chairs. The room was empty. "Lunch will be served there," said CFA Bruce.

They walked farther and heard voices.

"This is where the office staff sits," CFA Bruce explained.

"Hi, Liberty," a chorus of voices called out. "Hello, James."

Liberty and James said hi to the people they knew from back at the White House. People were typing on computers, talking into little recorder things, and snoozing. They walked farther toward the back.

"This is the guest section," CFA Bruce said, pointing to an empty area.

"Where are the guests?" Liberty asked.

"Right here." CFA Bruce pointed to James. "James is our honored guest today."

"Honor to be here." James bowed.

"Happy to have you," Liberty said. "Don't make me curtsy, though. I'll fall over."

Liberty walked back a little farther and saw a very familiar shiny head peeking over the seat. "SAM," she said. "Is this where you live?"

"For the next fourteen hours or so," SAM replied. "This is the agent section."

Liberty said hi to the other Secret Service agents. Then she leaned close to SAM and whispered in his ear. "The long hallway would be excellent for a red light, green light game."

"That might be a little too rambunctious, Rottweiler," he whispered back. "However, I'll challenge you to charades after lunch."

"Deal," Liberty agreed.

They continued the tour, walking to the back through a long, skinny corridor. CFA Bruce stopped to talk to someone about lunch.

"This hall would be an excellent place to practice cartwheels," Liberty said to James while they were waiting. "You'd have to get them perfectly straight."

"Cartwheels on the plane?" James said. "I'm not sure."

"It's smooth! Dare me?" Liberty asked him.

"No."

"Double dare me?"

"No," James said. "You should ask first. It might not be safe, plus I don't know if it's good manners to cartwheel around Air Force One."

"Erg," Liberty said, walking toward the back. "Sometimes you sound just like your mother. I can't always have perfect manners! And, ha, wait! Neither does your mother. At the young diplomats class, she *slurped* her soup. And *burped*!"

"My mother?" James looked surprised.

"I know!" Liberty said. "Everyone was, like, 'Mrs. Piffle slurped and burped!'"

Liberty was laughing so hard she didn't realize she had walked into the next room of the airplane. A bunch of men and women were sitting in their seats, with their laptops open. And their mouths open in surprise.

"Mrs. Piffle, chief of protocol, slurps and burps?" one of them asked.

"Liberty!" CFA Bruce came walking quickly behind them. "I wanted to let you know. This section is the press section."

Uh-oh. Liberty had accidentally walked into a press

section before. That time it was in her pajamas. She had embarrassed herself. Now she was embarrassing Mrs. Piffle! Liberty could just see the headlines:

"Please don't print that!" Liberty cried out. "I can explain!"

The reporters all started laughing.

"Don't worry," one reporter said. "We don't print what you say. It's off the record."

"We're reporters," another added. "Not Liberty re-Porters."

Phew!

"However, this could be an anonymous lead," another reporter said. "Just kidding!"

Liberty explained about the class and how Mrs. Piffle was showing what not to do. The reporters laughed with her, especially when she told them about the chocolate ice cream.

"You promise that's off the record?" Liberty double-checked.

"It's between you and us," a reporter said.

"Liberty, thanks for the entertainment," the reporters called. They all waved good-bye as she left the cabin.

"Now we can visit the presidential area of the plane. The president's suite is the private family quarters, where you can relax and rest. Some flights are very long, such as this one, so presidents can sleep on their flights comfortably," CFA Bruce said. "It's in the nose of the plane."

"We're going in the nose?" James asked. "I wonder if it's green. Get it? Green inside the nose?"

Liberty groaned at his bad joke. But then she laughed, because the president's suite *was* green!

It looked like a hotel room. There was a table and chairs and two beds and—

"Hey!" Liberty said. "Whose is that?"

"Whose do you think?" CFA Bruce smiled. "It's special for this trip."

One of the beds had a pink comforter on it and her beanie tiger, Mr. Fluffensauce! Liberty had her very own bed on Air Force One!

"Many presidents like to have their own special pillows with them or other things to make them feel comfortable," CFA Bruce said. "I know you like hard pillows and soft blankets."

"It's true!" Liberty clapped her hands. She went over and bounced on the bed. She saw some new books she wanted to read on the bookshelf and her favorite board game.

So cool!

"What's in this room?" Liberty asked, pointing to the door.

"The bathroom," CFA Bruce said. "It's empty."

"There's even a shower in there." Liberty went inside and peeked. And a potty. Airplane potties were always loud, but Liberty guessed Air Force One would have a super-potty that was super-quiet. She flushed.

FLUSSHHHWWWWRTHRP!!!!

"What was that?" James jumped. Oops, the potty was as loud as the ones on any other airplane.

"Just testing," Liberty said, embarrassed. She came out and flopped back on her bed. James was riding the exercise bike, which was like the one her parents used at home.

"This is so strange," James said, pedaling. "It doesn't seem like we're on an airplane."

"But we're forty-five thousand feet up in the sky," CFA Bruce said. "Over the Atlantic Ocean. Want to see?"

He flicked a switch, and the blinds over the windows raised up.

Liberty and James looked out the window. Yup, they were flying!

"But there's one more place you haven't seen."

"Where my parents are?" Liberty guessed.

"Exactly," CFA Bruce said. "They're in the president's office."

"Liberty! James! Come on in," her father called to them. He was sitting at a desk, working on a computer. Her mother was sitting on a couch, reading.

"How do you like the plane?" her dad asked.

"It's so cool!" Liberty and James both said.

"Is it time to do your schoolwork?" Liberty's father asked.

"You're probably right, sir," James replied.

Liberty groaned. They knew they had to do the schoolwork that they were missing. But *still*.

CFA Bruce stuck his head in. "Excuse me, lunch is being served," he said.

Saved!

President Porter, Mrs. Porter, Liberty, and James all went into the dining room. It was set with fancy plates and napkins that said AIR FORCE ONE.

"It's set so nicely, isn't it?" said Mrs. Piffle, coming into the room.

"It doesn't seem like we're on a plane, does it?" Liberty's mom asked. "It seems like we're in a restaurant, or even at home. Please join us, Mrs. Piffle."

They all sat down at the table. Liberty dug into the pilot's favorite grilled cheese. James ate his corn dog.

Liberty's father and Mrs. Piffle had the turkey sandwich, and her mother had the cheese and fruit plate.

"Delicious. They even brought my favorite mustard," the president said happily.

"Thank you for bringing me on this trip," James said.

"We're delighted to have you," Liberty's father answered. "It will be the first time in the country of Georgia for all of us."

"I've been reading up on Georgia," Liberty's mother said. "The country is about the size of our state of Georgia. We'll be visiting the capital, Tbilisi."

"Tee-bee-lee-see?" Liberty tried to pronounce it.

"Close," her father answered. "The *t* and *b* run together, so it's more like *Tb-lee-see*."

"The Georgians speak the Georgian language and also sometimes Russian," Liberty's mother explained.

"And English is becoming more and more commonly taught in schools."

"So I'll be able to talk to some people?" Liberty asked.

"Let's make sure you can talk to all people," her father answered. "Let's learn a few words in the Georgian language. "'Hello' is *gamarjoba*."

"Gah-mar-joe-ba," Liberty and James repeated.

"How about please and thank you?" James suggested. "My mother always says those are two of the most important words in any language."

"Your mother is right," President Porter said. "Please is *tu sheydzleba*, and thank you is *madlob*."

Liberty and James attempted to pronounce those. Liberty got "thank you" but mangled "please."

"We'll work on those later," Liberty's mom said.

"Do the Georgians know we're coming?" Liberty asked.

"Yes, and they're very excited to meet us," her father answered.

"I'm very excited to meet them," Liberty said. "This time I get to be the foreign special visitor."

Liberty thought about the time she had showed special foreign visitors around the White House. She had given them her special Porter Butter cookies, and later they had given her two sugar gliders.

"Oh no!" Liberty suddenly realized something. "We didn't bring any special gifts. Quick! Can we get some sugar gliders?"

"Sorry, no." Her mother laughed. "But don't worry, we did bring gifts."

"That's part of my mom's job," James said proudly.

"Yes, that is all taken care of," Mrs. Piffle said.

Liberty thought about it. James's mother had probably gotten gifts for the grown-ups in Georgia, but Liberty wanted to bring something for the kids.

What was something she could bring to show the kids of Georgia how excited she was to be visiting? Liberty thought about it while she was eating the Plane Vanilla Pudding CFA Bruce brought for dessert. She asked CFA Bruce if he had some supplies.

"Meet me in the conference room in five minutes," he told her.

After they had been excused, Liberty and James headed back to the conference room. CFA Bruce had really come through for them. Spread out on the floor was a ginormous piece of paper and a box of colored markers.

"We're going to make a sign," Liberty told James. "We can hold it up when we come out of the plane. I'll write 'People of Georgia' and you write '*gamarjoba*.'"

"How come I get the hard word?" James said.

"Um," Liberty said. "You get the hard word, but you also get the blue marker. Our favorite color!"

James seemed okay with that.

Liberty sat down and made big bubble letters. She still needed to color them in.

"This will take forever," she said. "We need to call in the troops." Liberty went to the back of the plane and rounded up SAM, another Secret Service agent, one secretary, a newspaper reporter, and a blogger. She assigned them each a red, black, pink, orange, and green marker.

"Ooh," the newspaper reporter said. "My pink marker smells like bubble gum."

"How come she got the scented marker?" joked the blogger.

They all colored in the giant bubble letters. Finally Liberty proclaimed the sign was ready to go.

They would make a grand and bubble-gum-scented entrance into the country of Georgia.

Chapter 8

LIBERTY WAS FLOATING OUT OF A CLOUD when she landed on the ground. She opened her backpack, and a gajillion sugar gliders flew out and glided around the country of Georgia.

". . . the country of Georgia," a voice said in the distance. "Liberty, wake up, we're almost in the country of Georgia."

Liberty opened her eyes and saw her mother standing over her, smiling. Liberty sat up in her bed and realized it wasn't her bed, it was Air Force One's bed in the presidential suite.

"Is it morning already?" Liberty asked. She had fallen asleep after:

- Playing charades with SAM, James, and Mrs. Piffle
- Playing Wii on the giant TV screen
- Making shadow puppets in the president's office with the lights out

And now they were landing!

She felt so glam. She was about to be Liberty Porter, International Girl!

"It's morning in Georgia," her mother answered. "There's a time difference, so in Georgia, it's already tomorrow morning."

"Whoa," Liberty said. "So at home it's still yester-day?"

Liberty got dressed in her special going-to-a-new-country-for-the-first-time-in-Air-Force-One dress. She fixed her hair and went out to meet her parents in her dad's office. Her mom and James were already there.

"Just in time." Her father smiled. "We're about to land."

Liberty sat down on the couch and buckled her seat belt. She felt the plane turn and then go down, down, down closer to the ground. She could see white, fluffy clouds out the window and then . . .

"Whoa!" Liberty and James both exclaimed. Out the window they could see huge mountaintops. Then Liberty could see lights in the distance.

"That's the city of Tbilisi," her father said. Liberty could see lots of buildings, houses, and a tall tower that was lit up with blinking lights. And next to it, also blinking blue, red, and green, was a big Ferris wheel.

Oh my gosh. Liberty was in a real live foreign country.

!!!!!!!

"James," his mother said. "You'll come with me out the back exit. Liberty and her parents will make their ceremonial debut out the front exit."

"Good luck!" James called to Liberty. "Don't forget to smile."

Liberty's mom did a last-minute patting down of Liberty's hair, and then they were ready. Liberty followed her parents and SAM up the aisle and to the door.

Liberty didn't need James to remind her she was about to enter a new country, or that she needed to smile—she was already smiling. But she suddenly felt nervous.

"I never went to a new country as First Daughter before," Liberty whispered to her father. "I never even went to a new country."

"Remember what I told you the first day of school," her father said. "Try your best."

"And you also reminded me not to wear pajamas," Liberty said.

"See, you're off to a good start already," her father said.

"And one, two, three. Mr. President, it's time," one of his people said.

Then the presidential music started, and someone announced "President William Porter of the United States of America." Liberty's father disappeared out the front exit. Liberty could hear cheers.

And then it was Liberty and her mother's turn. She held her mom's hand and stepped out onto the platform.

And then . . . Whoa!

Liberty saw a band playing horns and drums, and people waving American and Georgian flags. She watched in amazement as hundreds of soldiers in white uniforms marched up the tarmac and toward the plane.

"This is their honor guard," Liberty's father whispered to her.

"They're cool," Liberty said, as she watched them march around.

"Liberty Porter *es lamazia!*"

"Wait, that's me," Liberty said. "What does that mean?" A man in a suit came up and held out his hand.

"It means Liberty Porter is beautiful. Welcome to our country. I am the president of Georgia."

COOL! Liberty was meeting the president of another country IN his other country!

The president shook her hand. He had dark hair, a long coat, and movie-star sunglasses. Liberty opened her mouth to speak but suddenly felt very shy. So Liberty just smiled a big smile. Now she knew how other kids felt when they met her dad!

Then his wife introduced herself. She was very glamorous. Liberty got her voice back.

"*Gamarjoba*, Mrs. First Lady of Georgia," Liberty said.

"Welcome, welcome!" the First Lady said. "I see you are already learning our beautiful language."

"*Madlob!*" Liberty said. "Um, I forgot what that means, but *madlob*!"

"It means 'thank you.'" The First Lady smiled at her. "I look forward to seeing you again very soon."

Liberty thought that went well! The president and the First Lady talked to Liberty's mom and dad and then moved down the line.

"Liberty! Liberty!" a bunch of photographers started calling. Liberty smiled and waved to them.

She kept smiling and waving and was about to go down the stairs when she remembered something. Her sign!

"Sorry," she yelled to the crowd. "Forgot something important."

"Excuse me, excuse me." Liberty squeezed between a few Secret Service people and the pilot and found her rolled-up sign. She went back out to the top of the steps.

Then she turned to SAM. "Can you hold on to this for a second? Thanks."

SAM looked puzzled but took the edge of the paper. Liberty unrolled the sign with a flourish.

"Tada," Liberty said loudly. "*Gamarjoba*, people of Georgia! *Gamarjoba!*"

"*Gamarjoba!*" the reporters called back, and flash-bulbs went off everywhere.

Good news, Liberty thought. They seemed to like her welcome. She waved and waved as she followed

her parents down the steps and onto a red carpet.

A red carpet! Liberty felt like she was a movie star as she walked down the carpet waving at people, with flashbulbs going off.

A girl about Liberty's age came up and presented Liberty with an armful of flowers. She had long black hair with a bow on her head and was wearing a long, flowy red dress.

"Thank you," Liberty said. "These are *lamazia*."

The girl blushed.

"I'm Liberty," Liberty said. "What's your name?"

"I'm Nino," the girl said. "We are so excited to welcome you to Georgia."

They moved off to the side, while Liberty's father was greeting some people.

"You speak such great English," Liberty said.

"We learn it in school now," Nino explained.

"Maybe you can teach me some Georgian," Liberty said. "Do we get to hang out on this trip?"

Liberty hoped she would hang out with kids. It seemed like everyone else surrounding them was a grown-up in a suit. That could get BORING.

"I don't know," Nino answered.

"I'll ask my dad," Liberty said.

"This way, Liberty." Mrs. Piffle ushered her off the red carpet and into one of the black cars in the line.

"Hey," Liberty said, sliding into the seat. "This looks exactly like the Beast!"

The Beast was the nickname of the special presidential limo.

"That's because it *is* the Beast," her mother explained.

They'd brought the limo all the way to Georgia! Liberty's mom explained that the car goes wherever the president goes, anywhere in the world. And with it, the president's driver.

Oh yeah! Liberty could see the president's driver in the front seat sitting next to a Georgian official man. Liberty pressed a button to a speaker in the front.

"Hi, Kent!" Liberty said into the intercom. "*Gamarjoba*, Georgian man!"

"James and his mother will meet us at the embassy," her mother said.

"Very nice job on the sign, Liberty," her father complimented her.

Liberty beamed. She felt she was off to an excellent start in Georgia. She felt that way through the whole ride to her hotel, as she looked out the limo to see people on the streets waving to them.

"Hello! Hello, Georgia!" Liberty waved, even though she knew they couldn't see her. "Can't we at least beep a little to them?"

The driver honked the horn a few times. Liberty hoped the people knew that meant *Hi from Liberty Porter!*

"Tbilisi is a beautiful city," her mother said. "Look, that way there are tall mountains, but if you look out the other window, it looks like a busy city."

"Hey." Liberty pointed to a sign. "That's George Bush waving on that sign."

"Yes." Her father nodded. "The Georgians named a

big highway after our former president after he visited Tbilisi."

"Daddy, they might name a highway after you," Liberty said excitedly. "If they like you."

"I hope they like me," her father said.

"If not, they'll probably name an old building after you." Liberty laughed. "Or a pothole."

President Porter Pothole. Hee!

However, it would be cool to have a highway in another country named after you.

Liberty watched as they entered a new town with tall trees lining the streets and buildings with many balconies. Standing on the balconies were people waving and waving.

"The Georgian people love to have guests," the Georgian official told them. "Our country is famous for our hospitality."

"I can tell," Liberty said "Look at the signs."

Some people were waving signs that said USA. Others were waving American flags. It was very thrilling.

Liberty's father told her that they would have a visit at the United States embassy! He explained that an embassy is the official building of one country inside another country, where diplomats and other people work.

The motorcade pulled up to a large building.

"We'll have a quick meet and greet at the embassy," Mrs. Porter said. "That means we'll be meeting many American people who are living overseas and working here in Georgia, at our embassy."

The car stopped and the door opened, and suddenly Liberty was introduced to a blur of people: the ambassador to Georgia, who represents America; the deputy chief of mission, who is in charge at the embassy; and a bunch of grown-ups who worked at the embassy. Liberty shook a lot of hands.

"Now, Liberty, we'll introduce you to some fun people," the deputy chief of mission said, and winked at her. "Our kids. They're inside."

"Kids live at the embassy?" Liberty asked. The deputy chief of mission laughed.

"No, Liberty, they live in regular houses here in Tbilisi," he said. "Their parents work at the embassy, and we've all gathered here today to welcome you."

Liberty and her parents went inside to a big room, where a group of people were waiting. They all looked very excited to see the American visitors.

"Hello, Liberty!" they said.

"Hello, fellow American people also in the country of Georgia!" Liberty exclaimed.

Liberty wanted to say hi to the kids, but James's mother shushed her because it was speech time. Liberty sat on a chair and looked patriotical while people talked. Liberty's father talked and thanked all the embassy people for helping out both the American and Georgian countries, and for working and living here.

While he was talking, Liberty thought about what it would be like, not just to visit, but to live in a different country. Then finally her father stopped talking, and Liberty decided she could find out for herself.

Mrs. Piffle explained that her father would take pictures with each of the families. Liberty was welcome to say hello to them if she wanted to.

She wanted to! She wanted to find out what it was like to live in, not just visit, a different country. After the first family got their picture taken, Liberty said hi to their son.

"What's it like to live in a different country?" Liberty asked.

"Oh, we've lived in lots of different countries," the boy said. "I've lived in South Africa, Lithuania, Kyrgyzstan, and Australia."

"Oh my gosh," Liberty said. "That's so cool. I've only lived in America."

"Yeah, but you live in the White House," the boy said. "*That's* cool."

Liberty agreed. They were both lucky.

Liberty talked to all the kids after they had their picture taken with her dad. Some of them loved living overseas, and some of them didn't.

"The best part is meeting lots of people from different countries," one girl said. "There are people from all over the world at my school. The worst part is that there's no shopping mall here."

"The best part of living here," another boy said to Liberty, "is the food. It's delicious."

"But there's only one fast-food restaurant here," another girl said. "And they put mayonnaise on the hamburgers."

Liberty shuddered. She was not a fan of mayonnaise.

She found out that many of the kids lived in a compound with security guards and a pool. Some kids stayed for one year, some kids, a long, long time. Everybody was so interesting that Liberty was sad when it was time to go.

"Good-bye," she said to everybody. "Have fun living all over the world. Maybe I'll see you in another country."

Chapter 9

T HAT WAS FUN. I TALKED TO KIDS WHO have lived in countries I've never even heard of before," Liberty said, as her mother fixed her hair for the next event.

They were back at the hotel room, but only for a short amount of time.

"They are doing a great service for our country," her mother said.

"May I use that line in my next speech?" Liberty's father asked her as he straightened his tie. Then he kissed Liberty and her mother good-bye for a little while. He had some important meetings.

Liberty, James, and Liberty's mother were going to go sightseeing!

"What sights are we going to see?" Liberty asked.

"Let's just say it's time to put on a different outfit," Liberty's mother told her.

"Another dress? Something fancy?" Liberty asked.

"Actually, something that could get messy," Liberty's mother said, surprising her. "Jeans."

Messy? Jeans?

Liberty was still puzzling over it when they got into the car. First they drove through the city. Their car got to go straight through, with police cars with flashing lights leading the way.

"Look out for the Beast!" Liberty yelled. "The car! Not me! Heh!"

"Isn't it kind of crazy to have them stop traffic for you?" James said. "Your motorcade goes on for blocks."

"Really crazy," Liberty said. "I feel bad if someone is late for something. Unless it's a math test at school. Or the dentist. Then they're probably happy with me."

Their car drove along a little farther, and then they were leaving the city. Liberty could see a little village, and then suddenly the car came to a red light. And waited. And waited.

"They have really long red lights here," Liberty said.

"Oh, it's not a red light." The driver laughed. "Look out the front window."

Liberty looked and saw cows! Brown, black, and spotted cows were standing right in the middle of the road!

"That's so funny! There are cows blocking the road!" Liberty said, pointing out the window. Her mother and James looked.

"You don't see that in Washington, D.C.," Liberty's mother said.

"Happens all the time," the Georgian official said while the driver beeped the horn gently. "Sometimes sheep."

"Poor cows, just trying to walk somewhere, and the First Daughter and her motorcade come along and spoil everything," Liberty's mom said.

"It's a cow moo-torcade," James said.

"Please mooooove out of our way!" Liberty called out.

Finally they were out of cow jokes, and the cows were out of the road. They drove for a little while longer, and then the cars went out into a field, and everyone parked.

Liberty saw SAM and his people walking around, checking things out. She waved to SAM.

"Where are we?" Liberty asked. She stepped out of the car and saw what looked like miles of plants.

Then she saw the girl Nino and a tall man come toward her.

"Nino!" Liberty said. "I'm so happy to see you again!"

Nino stopped and kissed her on both cheeks as a greeting.

"Welcome to my uncle's vineyard!" Nino said. She introduced her uncle.

"Georgia is known for its vineyards dating back to 6000 BC," Nino's uncle said to them.

"Whoa," Liberty said. "They're old. And huge. What do you grow here?"

"Vineyards are for grapes." Nino laughed. "Georgia has more than five hundred different kinds of grapes. More than any other country in the world."

"I like grapes," Liberty said. "Can we eat them?"

"Sure," Nino said. "Taste a few. But too many will make you, how do you say it in English . . ."

She pantomimed "throw up."

"Throw up!" Liberty said. "Puke, lose your cookies, vomit."

"Regurgitate," James added.

"Okay, now I know." Nino laughed.

They each pulled a couple of grapes off the plants. *Mm.* They were juicy and delicious!

"And today we're going to put you to work," Nino's uncle said. "I know you *think* you are here on vacation, but we need some workers."

Liberty and James looked at each other and shrugged.

"Grab a bucket," Nino said. "And scissors. We're going grape picking."

Liberty had been apple picking in preschool. Pumpkin picking at Halloween. But never grape picking in a vineyard. Nino showed them how to look through the rows of vines to find juicy ones and then cut the grapes off the vine.

"Found some!" Liberty clipped some dark purple grapes off a vine and put them in a bucket.

"Got some!" James held up some green grapes.

"I got more," Liberty challenged James. "You got *nothing*."

"No, I got one, two, three." James was digging through his bucket. "Hang on, it's going to take a minute to count."

"James, that was a challenge," Liberty said. "You're supposed to say you got more. Then we get into a grape-picking competition."

"What about Nino?" James said. "Challenge Nino."

"It's Nino's vineyard." Liberty laughed. "I'm trying to win here. James, I'm going to take you down. You are going to lose, with a capital *L*."

James sighed.

"Okay. Nino, can you be referee?"

Nino nodded.

"Ertee," Nino said. *"Oree, sah-mee."*

"GO!" James and Nino both shouted.

Wait, what? What just happened? Liberty got it a minute too late. James took off into the vines.

"Oh, she was doing one, two, three, go!" Liberty said. "That was tricky!"

"Just trying to win here," James yelled back.

"Not bad," Liberty said. "I like your spirit."

Then she focused on picking the grapes. *Clip! Clip! Clip!*

"Smile," her mom said, holding up a camera.

"No distractions, Mom!" Liberty said. She was cutting purple grapes! Green grapes! Her bucket was slowly filling up, closer to the top, closer and—

"Finished!" James said. He held up his bucket— overflowing with grapes.

"James is the grape-picking winner!" Nino announced.

"Argh!" Liberty yelled. "I was so, so close."

"I win! I am the winner!" James yelled. "Grape champion of the world!"

"Wow, I've never seen James so competitive," Liberty said to her mother. They watched as he ran around the vineyard with his hands raised in victory and came up to them.

"I crushed you like a grape," James said to Liberty. "Get it? Crushed like a grape?"

"I think you've created a monster," Liberty's mother whispered to Liberty.

"No kidding," Liberty agreed.

"What's the next competition?" James asked. "I'm on a roll!"

"No, for the next one we need to work together," Nino said. "Teamwork."

Liberty put her grape bucket down.

"Oh, you'll need those grapes," Nino said, smiling. She pointed up a tall hill. "We'll be bringing the grapes up there."

Liberty looked down at her pail of grapes, which was already feeling pretty heavy. The thought of carrying them up the hill was *whew!* tiring. Suddenly she was glad she had not picked as many grapes as James. His bucket was going to be seriously heavy to carry up that hill. Liberty picked up her bucket and started to walk.

"Oh, Liberty, we are not walking," Nino said. "Here comes our ride."

They heard a rumbling noise, and then a large pickup truck pulled up close. It was driven by the same farm worker who'd been with Nino earlier.

"Jump on," Nino said.

"We'll meet you kids up top," Liberty's mother said.

"It's like a hayride," Liberty said, climbing on the back, "except instead of hay, there are grapes."

And boy, were there grapes. There must have been sixteen billion green and purple grapes in boxes almost filling up the back of the truck. There was just enough room for Liberty, James, and Nino to have a seat.

"I thought I picked a lot of grapes," James said, "but suddenly my bucket looks pretty lame."

"We have many expert grape pickers in the vineyard." Nino smiled. "I'm sure with practice you would become an expert too."

The driver started the pickup, and *bumpety-bump-bump-bump*, they went up the hill with the grapes. The truck stopped at the top of the hill. The kids got off and went over to where a man was there to greet them.

Nino introduced them to her uncle Dato.

"He doesn't speak English," Nino explained, "but he welcomes you as our honored guests to the vineyard."

"*Gamarjoba*," Liberty said to him. Then she leaned toward Nino and whispered, "Did I do that right?"

"Excellent," Nino responded.

Liberty looked at James, waiting for his usual perfectly polite hello.

But James didn't say hello. What James did do was yell, "Beast!"

And run. And run and run.

Chapter 10

THE BEAST?" LIBERTY LOOKED AROUND. Why was James scared of the presidential limo?

"Uh," she said, watching James run back to the pickup and jump in the back. "Sorry . . . um . . ."

Uncle Dato shrugged and said something in Georgian to Nino.

"Do you know what happened?" Liberty asked Nino.

"I'm not sure," Nino said.

They turned to look at James, who was sitting on the truck bed and waving frantically to them.

Nino looked puzzled too. Then her eyes widened.

"Oh!" she said. "I think James meant *that*."

She pointed to something that was peeking out from behind a large shed.

"It *is* a beast," Liberty breathed.

"No, that is my uncle's dog!" Nino laughed.

"That's a dog? It looks like a bear," Liberty said. That dog was the biggest dog she had ever seen in her life. It was white and shaggy and just . . . huge.

"This is Gogo, which means girl," Nino translated. "She is a Caucasian Mountain dog. The Caucasus are the mountains around us. These dogs are wonderful protectors. Some of these dogs are not friendly, but Gogo is."

"I wonder if James will believe that. He is . . . sensitive about dogs," Liberty said. Then she called to James, "It's a dog! A friendly dog."

James still didn't move.

Nino whistled and Gogo came over. Nino petted her.

Then Gogo came up to Liberty. Liberty stood very still.

Gogo sniffed at her. Then the dog rubbed her massive

head against Liberty's leg.

"She's so sweet," Liberty said. "I need to tell James."

She walked up to James, who was sitting high up in the truck bed.

"It's a dog," Liberty said again. "And she's friendly."

James shook his head.

"Really, she's nice and—"

"AH!" James interrupted her with a yelp.

Liberty didn't know that Gogo had followed her up to the pickup. And now she was going up the steps, up, up, up to James.

"AHHHH!" James tried to climb higher up on the crates of grapes.

"James! You'll squish the grapes!" Liberty said. "Gogo! Come here!"

Gogo wasn't listening. The giant dog was looking around as if she was trying to find something.

"Grr," she growled softly.

"What?" James yelled. "Why is she growling at me?"

"She's not growling *at* you," Nino said.

Liberty realized she was right when Gogo circled around James. He inched away from her to the other side of the truck bed.

"Gogo knows you're a friend," Nino said. "She wants to protect you."

"She wants to protect me from what?" James said. "I'm trying escape from *her*!"

James moved backward and tried to sit on the pile of grapes.

"She knows you are afraid of something," Nino said. "She is trying to find it and then protect you."

"Ah!" James slid down the crates of grapes and landed on his back.

And that was when it happened.

Gogo went over and started licking James on the cheek.

"Get it off me!" James yelped. "Get it—oooph."

Gogo rested her head on James's shoulder. He wiggled away. But she wiggled closer and snuggled up next to him. Then she nuzzled him.

"Wow, she really likes you," Nino said.

"Oh, that's so sweet," Liberty said. "I think. Are you okay under there?"

James seemed to have stopped wiggling.

"Hm," James said. "She's very warm. And cozy."

That was when Liberty saw James lift his arm and put it around Gogo.

"She is kinda like my warm, fuzzy blanket I had when I was two," he mumbled.

"Did James just say the dog was like his warm, fuzzy blanket?" Liberty whispered to Nino.

"I think so," Nino said.

Uncle Dato walked up and said something to Nino.

"Aah, he says we are ready," Nino translated.

"Ready for what?" Liberty asked.

"Our next fun," Nino said. "We have to follow Uncle Dato."

"Okay, James," Liberty called to him. "We have to leave."

"Mmphff," said James.

"James, we have to go," Liberty said louder.

"Mmphff," he said louder.

He didn't move. His arms stayed wrapped around the big dog.

Gogo sighed happily.

"I think your friend James is not so afraid anymore," Nino said.

James wasn't afraid anymore! He was so NOT afraid, he didn't want to leave the dog.

"She's so warm and cuddly," he said.

Uncle Dato said something to Nino.

"Uncle Dato says the dog can come with you," Nino said.

James sat up. He carefully patted Gogo on the head.

"You can come with me," he said to the dog. And they both climbed out of the truck bed and started following Uncle Dato, Liberty, and Nino.

"I can't believe you're not afraid of dogs anymore," Liberty said to James.

"I'm never afraid," James said, glancing at Nino. "Just sensitive."

"Well then, I can't believe you're not sensitive to the biggest, hugest dog that's practically a bear," Liberty said. "Impressive."

Gogo stayed by James's side the entire time. Liberty noticed he scratched her massive head a couple of times.

She smiled. Then she stopped smiling and looked confused. Uncle Dato had stopped in front of a giant wooden tub.

Why was there a tub out here?

"A tub?" Liberty said. "Are we taking baths? Does it have a Jacuzzi?"

"It's not a bathtub." Nino laughed. "Watch what we put inside."

Uncle Dato started picking up crates of grapes from the tractor and dumping them into the tub. Soon the tub was filling up with hundreds of grapes.

Gogo sniffed around the tub at all the grape smells.

"Imagine taking a bath in that." Liberty laughed.

"Oh, you don't have to imagine it," Nino said. "Hop on in."

"Seriously?" Liberty asked. She looked at James. He looked at her.

"Does my mother know about this?" Liberty asked, looking at the mess in the bottom.

"She did say wear clothes that can get messy," James reminded her.

"Well, you're not exactly taking a bath," Nino explained, "but you are going to do the traditional Georgian grape stomp. Wash your feet in that bucket of water and prepare to stomp."

So cool. Liberty and James took off their shoes. They stepped into the bucket of water.

"Now, Mr. SAM," Nino said, "would you please drop Liberty into the grapes?"

SAM picked Liberty up and put her into the tub so she was standing on grapes.

EEWWW! SQUISHY! Cold grapes were squishing between Liberty's toes!

"Liberty Porter, First Daughter, Feet Juice!" James said. "The newest drink sensation."

"Come on in, James!" Liberty called to him.

"Umm." James looked unsure. "Feet? Grapes? How does it feel?"

"Squishy," Liberty said, "cold, squishy, gooey,

kinda disgusting, and really awesome."

Before James could say anything, SAM had picked him up and plopped him into the tub of grapes.

"You are making grape juice," Nino said, clapping her hands.

"We are?" Liberty asked. She looked over the side of the tub, where Nino was pointing. She was right. Grape juice was pouring out of a spout.

"The more you stomp, the more juice you make," Nino said.

"Juice?" James looked horrified. "We're not going to have to drink feet juice, are we?"

"We will not be serving this feet juice." Nino smiled. "We are here for the fun of the stomp."

"Stomp, James!" said Liberty. "Stomp!"

James took a tentative step. "It feels so squeezy," he said. Then he lifted his other foot and stomped. Then a grin spread across his face.

"You're right," he said. "This is disgusting, and awesome."

Liberty stomped and stamped her feet. The grapes squished under her feet and between her toes. James was stamping away.

"Hey, wait," Liberty said. "Nino, climb in and stomp with us."

"Oh, I shouldn't," Nino said.

"Oh, you should," Liberty insisted.

"Come on," James said.

Nino washed her feet and climbed in too. The three of them stomped and stamped. Liberty marched. James tap-danced. Liberty did the chicken dance.

"Woo-hoo!" Liberty yelled. And then she stopped.

"SAM!" Liberty called out. "Come here!"

"Are you ready to get out, Liberty?" SAM asked.

"No," Liberty said, "but you're ready to get in!"

"Oh, I can't, I'm on duty," SAM said with a smile. "I'm the only agent here and—"

"No, you're not!" Liberty pointed behind him.

Liberty's mother and her two Secret Service agents were heading their way.

"Well now, this looks fun," Liberty's mother said, and peered into the grape tub. "What purple feet you have, Liberty."

"I know, right?" Liberty said, lifting her foot. It was purple practically to her knee. "We're making feet juice," she said. "SAM was just about to join us."

"Oh no, no, no," SAM protested.

"Oh, yes, yes, yes," the other Secret Service agents chimed in. Then they all started chanting, "SAM! SAM! SAM! SAM!"

SAM reached down and untied his shiny shoes. Then he took off his long black socks.

"This is so great," James said under his breath.

SAM rolled up his suit pants and climbed into the grape-filled tub.

"Stamp, SAM!" Liberty yelled. SAM gently stepped on the grapes a few times, then started to grin. And he stomped.

Stomp, stomp! Stamp, stamp! Squoosh, squoosh!

First Lady Porter took out her camera phone and took a picture.

"James, Liberty, Nino, and SAM feet juice," she said.

"Truly disgusting." SAM laughed.

"Truly awesome," Liberty agreed.

James stuck his grapey foot out of the tub, and Gogo licked it. Truly disgustingly awesome.

Chapter 11

LIBERTY WAS BACK IN THE TUB. THIS TUB was not nearly so fun, because it was a regular bathtub at her hotel.

"Are you still purple?" her mother called to her.

Liberty stuck her toes out of the water and checked. More like a pale lavender.

"Mostly not," she called back. She scrubbed her feet until they were back to normal.

When Liberty was done, she came out to see her mother, all dressed up for a fancy dinner.

Mrs. Porter was holding a fancy dress out to her.

It was black and silky and poofed out at the bottom.

"A Georgian clothes designer made you something to wear tonight," her mother said. "Isn't it lovely?"

Liberty put it on and felt like a princess. Then her mother tied a matching bow in her hair. There was a knock on the door.

"Are you ladies ready?" her father's voice called.

Liberty and her mother went out to meet her father and James in the suite. Her father and James were both dressed up for dinner too.

"Will Nino be able to come to dinner too?" Liberty asked.

"Yes," her father said. "Nino's father is one of our hosts of the *supra*."

"What's a *supra*?" Liberty asked.

"It's the traditional dinner," her father said, smiling. "You will have to wait and see for yourself. The *supra* will be at the president of Georgia's house."

They drove to the president's house.

"Hey, it's white like our house!" Liberty said.

"Now, I'm sure I don't need to remind you two to be on your best behavior," President Porter said.

"My mother has been training me for this moment since I was born," James said dramatically.

"Oh please," Liberty muttered.

"I'm glad James appreciates what a special occasion this is," Mrs. Piffle said. "And that you two got your sillies out this afternoon at the grape stomp."

Liberty knew it was a special occasion. She would be on her very, very best behavior. She planned to be absolutely perfect.

She felt very excited and a little nervous as she went into the president's house. It was funny to think that other people might feel nervous when they visited her house.

There was a lot of shaking hands, many hellos,

many *gamarjoba*s. James had to go off with his mother somewhere, while Liberty did First Daughterly stuff.

And then Liberty was standing in front of the First Lady of Georgia.

"*Gamarjoba*, First Lady of Georgia," Liberty said.

"*Gamarjoba*, First Daughter of the United States," the First Lady said, and smiled. She was very glamorous.

Liberty suddenly felt starstruck.

"Some people call me FDOTUS," she blurted out. "I know it sounds silly."

The First Lady of Georgia laughed. "Then I suppose that would make me FLOG." Now they both laughed.

Then Liberty was introduced to the president of Georgia. She used her most excellent manners. And she was relieved that she did not have to curtsy.

"I would like to show you a lovely view of the city," the POG told them.

They went up a staircase made of glass and into

a room that was practically all glass too.

They could see the city lights and the mountains. Liberty thought about how far away she was from home. Then she looked up into the sky and saw the stars twinkling.

"Isn't it incredible," Liberty's father said, "to think that even though we're halfway around the world, people in America can look up and see the very same stars in the sky?"

"Yes, yes, we have the same sky," everyone was murmuring. "So true."

"Umm." Liberty cleared her throat. "Except, Daddy, it's daytime in America. So nobody there is actually looking at the stars right now."

People looked at Liberty.

"Umm, they're in school and stuff right now," she added.

"Yes, it's true," the president of Georgia said with a

laugh. "She is right. She is a very smart First Daughter."

"Yes, she is." Her father chuckled. He smoothed down Liberty's hair and smiled at her proudly. "Yes, she is."

They all went back down the glass staircase.

"Liberty, why don't you spend some time with James while your father and I mingle?" Liberty's mother said to her. Liberty skipped over to where James was standing with his mother.

"You have been wonderful on this trip," Mrs. Piffle said. "I'm proud of both of you."

"James has been an excellent influence," Liberty agreed. "Good thing he was here, or who knows what manners I would have goofed up."

"It was fun!" James said. "Meeting everyone, the grape stomp, now the *supra* . . . except . . ."

James suddenly looked sad.

"I miss Gogo," he said quietly.

"You miss going where?" Mrs. Piffle looked concerned.

"I miss Gogo," James repeated. "The dog I met at the grape stomp."

"You're missing a dog? But you're sensitive to dogs!" Mrs. Piffle said.

"Oh, this wasn't just any dog," Liberty chimed in. "Gogo was like hugging a giant bear of softness."

"Gogo is tough and strong and protects people," James said. "I just wish she could come with us."

He looked sadder than Liberty had ever seen him. Really, really sad.

"James, you don't care for dogs," Mrs. Piffle said. "And dogs shed and leave little hairs all over the house. They make messes. And they have terrible manners when they eat, and they greet people by jumping up on them."

"I know." James sighed.

Mrs. Piffle gave him a hug.

"You can play with Franklin when we get home," Liberty told him.

"Thanks," James said. "I will."

Well, that was something else good from this trip! James wasn't so sensitive to dogs. And it was all thanks to a dog that was so hugenormous that even Liberty was "sensitive" to her at first.

"Are you enjoying your time here, Liberty?" the president of Georgia asked her.

"Yes sir, definitely. There are lots of great things," Liberty said. "Like the grape stomp. And meeting people. And my friend likes dogs!"

"Well." The president of Georgia looked a little confused. "I am happy you enjoyed the day. And that your friend likes dogs. Now there is more enjoyment to come."

He led the way out of the room and down a hall.

"You told the president you were happy that I like dogs?" James whispered to Liberty, as they were walking.

"Well, it's a big deal," Liberty insisted.

She followed her parents, James, SAM, and the president of another country(!) into the dining room. Inside it was a ginormously long table that was pretty much groaning with food.

"Whoa!" Liberty said out loud.

"Whoa?" The POG turned to her and smiled.

"I've never seen so much food in my entire life," Liberty said.

"This?" The president waved his hand. "This is simply the first starter course! I hope you like to eat."

Did Liberty Porter like to eat? Oh, Liberty Porter definitely liked to eat!

Chapter 12

T HERE'S MORE FOOD COMING," JAMES whispered.

"Whoa," Liberty said again.

A woman introduced herself as the chief of protocol.

"That's what James's mother does!" Liberty blurted out.

The woman came over to James. He held out his hand and shook hers formally.

"I will tell your mother you have a wonderful handshake," the woman said to James.

"*Didi madloba*," James responded. "Thank you very much."

"Your mother is going to be so happy," Liberty whispered to James.

The chief of protocol seated them at the table. Liberty was across from her parents, who were sitting next to the president of Georgia. On Liberty's left side was James, but the right side was empty—for a moment.

Then somebody slid into the seat next to her—Nino!

"Nino!" Liberty clapped her hands. "You're here! And I love your dress!"

"Thank you!" Nino replied.

Liberty scoped out the food. There were many small plates, meant to be passed and shared. One plate had pink blobs, green blobs, and brown blobs, arranged nicely, but they just looked strange.

"Are you okay?" James whispered. "You're making a weird face."

"Oops!" Liberty pasted on a smile and whispered to Nino.

"What is that, and that . . . and that?"

"You're probably thinking they look like blobs," Nino said quietly.

They are actually quite tasty. They're called *pkhali.*"

"Puh-khalee," Liberty repeated. They had walnuts and a grape paste inside them. Interesting.

"We can start with something to drink," Nino said. "Would you prefer pear, lemon, grape—"

"Not grape," Liberty accidentally blurted out. All she could think of was that she might be drinking feet juice.

"It's *not* your feet juice," Nino responded, reading her mind. "But if you'd like to try something other than grape, how about pear juice?"

Liberty took a sip.

Hm! Pretty good! Different! And then, speaking of different, everyone started putting blobs and sprigs on their plates.

It was time to start eating. James took a big bite of a green blob.

"This is good," he said.

"Try the purple," Liberty's mother suggested. "It's wonderful."

Liberty put one tine of a fork into a purple blob. She tried a teeny, teeny taste.

Bleh. She did not think it was so wonderful.

"Very polite cover-up," James whispered.

"Thanks," Liberty said after gulping down some neon green soda that was in another glass by her plate to get rid of the taste. The soda tasted strange . . . almost spicy.

"That's tarragon soda," James said.

Tarragon? Liberty wasn't even sure what that was.

She was starting to wonder if there was anything familiar on the table.

"I know you'll like this," James said, seeing the look on Liberty's face and pointing at a plate of bread covered with cheese.

Liberty took a slice of the cheese bread.

James was right. It was yum.

"I bet Cheese Fries would like this," Liberty said to James.

She munched on the bread and watched as her parents, the Georgian president, and other important-looking adults talked and munched up and down the huge, long table.

Suddenly the president of Georgia stood up, holding a glass. The room fell silent.

"My friends," the POG said. "I wish to welcome our American guests: President Porter of the United States, the First Lady of the United States, the First Daughter of the United States, and the First Friend of the First Daughter of the United States."

"Hey, that's me," James whispered, pleased.

"To our friendship . . ."

The POG talked and talked and talked. Liberty looked around the table and thought about how amazing it was that she was here in a different country, with all these people from a different country . . . and drinking a really, really green soda.

After the POG spoke, everyone raised their glasses and said, *"Gaumarjos!"*

"Gaumarjos!" Liberty said as she clinked glasses with James, her mother, Nino, the president of the United States, and the president of Georgia.

More food was brought to the table. Now the table was seriously groaning with food. Liberty's plate of goop was whisked away and replaced with a clean plate waiting for the next round.

"This is my favorite dish," Nino said, pointing to a platter of chicken in a delicious garlic sauce.

Liberty agreed. The chicken was delicious. She had barely finished it when her plate was once again cleared away.

Then the next course was brought out. And unfortunately, it was placed directly in front of Liberty.

Unfortunately, because it was a fish. Not just fish, but a fish with its head still on.

Yeeps! Liberty tried not to look at the fish.

Its googly eyes were staring right at Liberty. But nobody else noticed, because everybody else was watching another important-looking Georgian person, who was giving another toast about their wonderful countries.

"Blah blah blah . . . ," was all Liberty heard, because she could not stop staring at or smelling the fish on the plate.

She tried to kick James under the table. But she missed and kicked the table leg. The table shook, making the fish on the plate shake and look like it was alive.

Yeeps!

Liberty was running out of self-control.

Suddenly she had a horrible thought. What if she had to eat the ugly, staring fish? What if it was an important tradition to eat the ugly, staring fish face?

Liberty started to squirm in her seat, just as the toast ended and everybody clinked glasses.

"Dig in!" somebody said.

Liberty held her breath and prepared to eat the ugly fish head.

"Oh no, the fish is in front of Liberty," Nino said. "Perhaps we should move that a little farther away."

Liberty almost fell off her chair in relief.

"Do I have to eat that thing?" she whispered to Nino.

"Of course not," Nino reassured her. "You might wish to try this instead."

"Yum, meat on a stick," James said happily. "Everything thing tastes better when it's on a stick!"

Liberty perked up and slid the piece of yummy-looking meat onto her plate.

She focused on that and not on her father, who was eating the ugly fish.

Shudder.

Liberty enjoyed the meat on a stick, more cheesy bread, fried potatoes, and beans. James's favorite was a clay pot filled with mushrooms, which sizzled loudly in front of them. Liberty liked the sizzle, but she didn't like mushrooms.

More people gave toasts, and glasses were clinking away.

Liberty ate more cheesy bread until she thought she was going to explode. She slumped in her seat.

"I am so stuffed," she groaned to Nino. "I don't think I could even stand up."

"Oh, you will have to soon," Nino said.

Before she had a chance to explain, music began to play.

"The entertainment!" POG announced.

Suddenly a group of dancers leaped into the room.

The women were wearing long dresses. The women's hair was worn in long braids.

"Our traditional dance," Nino said proudly.

Liberty watched the women glide beautifully.

"The women are so graceful," she said. "I think their hands float like fluttering birds."

"I take dance lessons at school," Nino said. "Some-day I wish to dance like that."

The music got dramatically loud. Then six men burst into the room and leaped over toward the women. The men were wearing black and red long jackets. They wore tall, fuzzy hats on their heads.

Liberty had never seen anything like it. The men danced powerfully. Their legs were bending in ways Liberty never thought possible.

"How do they do that?" James wondered.

Everyone at the table began to clap to the beat. Liberty grinned and clapped too. *Clap. Clap. Clap.*

They clapped faster and faster as the dancers whirled and twirled and lunged and leaped around the dinner table.

And then one of the dancers leaped over in front of Liberty and held out his hand to her.

Liberty shook it. He shook his head and pulled her right off her chair.

"Dance, Liberty!" Nino said.

"It's not a real event until the children dance!" POG announced grandly.

"Me? Dance?" Liberty looked around.

It seemed like everybody was staring at her.

Liberty suddenly felt the pressure.

"I can't dance like that," she said quietly through clenched teeth to Nino.

"She can't," James agreed.

"Gee, thanks, James," Liberty told him.

"Just feel the music," Nino said.

Liberty allowed the dancer to lead her to the front of the room, where all the dancers were smiling at her. She stood stiffly, feeling all the eyes in the room watching her.

Then one of the women dancers took Liberty's hand and started to guide her hand, as it fluttered through the air.

Liberty felt a teeny bit graceful. She pointed her toe the way her ballet teacher from when she was four had tried to show her.

And as the music played, the audience clapped.

Liberty started to dance.

"Go, Liberty!" she heard James cheer.

Liberty could even see SAM standing off to the side of the room, giving her a thumbs-up.

"All the children dance!" proclaimed the chief of protocol.

Then the dancers leaped and twirled off the dance floor and went to the table. One took Nino's hand and another grasped James's.

Ha! James had to dance too!

James stumbled up to the dance floor. He froze for a moment. Then he got down on one knee and then another. And then he leaped. And he lunged. He took the hands of one of the women dancers and twirled her around.

"Go, James!" Liberty cheered him on.

"My mom made me take ballroom dancing," James told her as he leaped by.

"Impressive," Nino noted.

Liberty, James, Nino, and all the dancers danced until the song ended. The room burst into applause.

Liberty started to head back to her seat.

"Oh, *ara, ara, ara*! No no, no!" the POG protested.

"We are not done with our dance." The POG extended his hand to Liberty's mother and escorted her to the dance floor. One of the flowy women dancers went and whisked Liberty's father out to the dance floor.

"Dad," Liberty whispered to him, "just kind of do your robot!"

"Got it." Her father nodded.

The music began.

The First Lady twirled, Liberty whirled, James leaped, and Liberty's father busted out his herky-jerky robot.

And everybody danced.

Chapter 13

"THE *SUPRA* WAS SO MUCH FUN!" LIBERTY said the next day. It had lasted late into the night. Liberty had also felt jet-lagged from the long trip, so she had slept practically until lunch.

"I'm glad you had fun," her mother said, "but this afternoon we have some official duties."

"Official, like in 'boring meeting' official?" Liberty asked. She knew her father had gotten up early to go to some meetings where grown-ups would just blah blah blah talk.

"I know we are greeting some Georgian children and their families," her mother said.

"Okay, good, that won't be boring," Liberty said.

Later that afternoon Liberty, her mother, James, SAM, and his crew were ushered downstairs to the door of a big ballroom.

"Welcome," said a woman in a gray suit, who came up and introduced herself as the host of this special event. She introduced a man as a television reporter, and Liberty looked behind him and saw some people holding cameras.

"We will be filming the First Lady's speech for our country's news," the television reporter explained.

Liberty's mom winked at her. Liberty was grateful for the heads-up. She would make sure not to itch her nose or yawn during her mother's speech. Not that her mother's speeches were boring, but okay, sometimes they were.

"We hope you have felt very welcome in our country," the woman said.

"Definitely," Liberty told her.

"And we hope this will make you feel even more welcome." The woman opened the door to the ballroom, and Liberty heard cheering.

"Hello! Hello!"

Liberty followed the woman into the ballroom and saw hundreds of cheering kids and grown-ups—there was even a local band playing the national anthem! When they saw Liberty, they went wild.

"Hello, Liberty Porter!" they yelled, *"Garmarjoba!"*

"Hello, people of Georgia!" Liberty called back, and waved and waved. They were all waving at Liberty, her mother, and James. It was very exciting.

Liberty followed the host and Mrs. Porter up the steps to a stage. They showed Liberty to a chair where she would sit while her mother gave the speech.

While her mother was speaking, Liberty looked out over the audience. And around the audience, where there were huge screens showing her mother onstage talking so people in the back could see.

And that meant there was a giant Liberty onscreen too. She was sitting behind her mother. Liberty moved her hand. Giant Liberty onscreen moved her hand. Liberty squirmed. Giant Liberty squirmed too. Awkward.

Liberty decided to ignore the Giant Liberty. She would look at the audience instead. She tried to smile at as many kids as she could. They looked just like the kids from home. Liberty thought about how weird it was to be halfway across the world but the kids looked just like the kids at home.

Liberty caught the eye of one girl, who smiled excitedly at her. Then Liberty caught the eye of a boy, who crossed his eyes at her.

Wait, did he just cross his eyes at her? Liberty did a double take, and he *was* crossing his eyes at her. And now he was making a funny face.

Yup, the kids here were just like the kids at home. That boy was probably just like Max Mellon. Liberty used all her self-control not to cross her eyes back at him.

Then she heard her mother say, "Liberty Porter, my daughter."

She focused back on her mother, who was pointing at Liberty. Liberty smiled and waved.

"Perhaps Liberty would like to say a few words," the host said into the microphone.

Um. Uh.

Liberty looked at her mom.

"Excuse us one moment," her mom said, and came over to her. The host started talking about "Gogo." Liberty remembered that the dog's name meant "girl."

"You don't have to say anything," her mom whispered.

Then they heard chanting. "Lib-er-ty! Lib-er-ty!"

"I'll do it," Liberty said.

"Remember, they're filming for TV," her mother said.

The TV show would be broadcast throughout the whole country of Georgia.

"But wait, what am I supposed to say?"

"You may say whatever you feel," Liberty's mother said. "I trust you."

Her mother trusted her! Her mother trusted her to represent their family on live TV! To represent *America* on live TV! Not to embarrass herself, and embarrass herself on . . . *live* . . . *TV*.

Liberty suddenly felt a little sickish in her stomach. Live TV made her suddenly very, very nervous.

But then she heard voices calling out.

"Liberty! Liberty!!!"

She took a deep breath and walked out onto the stage. The audience started clapping and whistling and cheering.

"Hi," Liberty said nervously into the microphone. "No, wait, wait, I mean, *GAMARJOBA!*"

Now the audience really went wild!

"*Gamarjoba*, Liberty," the people were calling. "*Gamarjoba!*"

"I am so happy to be here, in your country!" Liberty said. "This is my first trip to a different country as a First Daughter. Everybody has been *sooo* nice!"

The interpreter repeated what Liberty said in Georgian. The audience smiled at her.

Liberty looked over to her mother. Her mother was smiling too. Liberty saw SAM give her a thumbs-up. Yay, Liberty thought, this was going great!

"I got to stomp on grapes and make feet juice,"

Liberty said. "I got to go to a *supra*! I got to eat your cheese bread. I got to dance with Georgian dancers!"

Liberty looked straight into the TV camera and prepared for a perfect finish to her speech. She thought about the Georgian words that Nino had taught her. She tried to remember and . . .

Liberty pointed at the audience for her big finish. She thought about how her father always had a great last line to make the crowd cheer.

"So I want to say this to all of you. Someday I want to have a *supra* with all of you! *Me supra tvalis gugas!*"

Suddenly the crowd gasped. The cheering turned to mumbles and mutters.

Uh-oh.

Liberty's mother put her face in her hands. And then the crowd burst out laughing. Liberty stood frozen.

The host came up and placed her hand on Liberty's shoulder.

"Didn't I say, 'I want to eat with all of you boys and girls'?" Liberty whispered.

"Not exactly," the host whispered back. "You just told everybody that you will feast on their eyeballs!"

Chapter 14

LIBERTY FELT HER FACE TURN BEET RED. She saw everyone staring at her and laughing. She fled off the stage.

Liberty ran into the empty waiting room. She felt humiliated and pretty much a big stupid dummy head. She had told the audience she would eat their eyeballs! And not just the audience, but everyone on TV!

"Liberty," SAM said, coming quickly into the room.

"Liberty, are you okay?" her mom said.

She shook her head no. She tried to hold back her tears, but she had a big lump in her throat.

"Liberty," her mother said, kneeling down next to her. "You have to stop being so hard on yourself!"

"I messed it up. I wanted to represent America," Liberty choked. "Now they think I'm going to eat their eyeballs."

Liberty thought about how Max Mellon told her she would embarrass herself by sneezing on TV. This was even worse. Duh, a girl is *gogo*, not *guga*! How could she be so dumb?

"Oh, Liberty, you know we all make our mistakes!" her mother said.

"On TV?" Liberty asked.

SAM coughed.

"If I may interrupt," SAM said. "I have an embarrassing TV moment. My first job was protecting a congresswoman, and it was very hot. When I saw her speech on TV later, there was a glare reflecting a bright light. It kept distracting her during the speech."

"So what?" Liberty asked.

"It was my shiny bald head," SAM admitted. "The other agents called me Shiny SAM and Slippery SAM and Sweaty SAM. . . ."

Liberty could not help it. She started to laugh. Then she groaned.

"Oh no. People will call me Eat your Eyeballs Porter."

"There certainly have been more embarrassing moments," said Liberty's mother. "One president threw up at dinner on the prime minister of Japan."

"Seriously?" Liberty said.

"Yes, right on his lap."

"Oh," Liberty said. "That *is* more embarrassing."

The door opened and Nino burst in.

"Liberty," she said, "aren't you coming back out? The children are waiting for you!"

"Waiting for me to eat their eyeballs?" Liberty asked.

"Don't be silly," Nino said. "Everybody loved that you tried to talk with us in our language!"

"But I screwed up!" Liberty cried. "What's worse than telling them I will eat their eyeballs?"

"Liberty, we have a good sense of humor!" Nino said. "The interpreter explained you didn't mean that. Only a few children ran away crying."

"Oh no," Liberty said.

"I'm teasing you!" Nino said. "I joke. Nobody ran. Plus it will be a funny story to be told at *supras* for the years to come. Perhaps we will say 'Cheers to our good friend Liberty Porter, who will eat our eyeballs!'"

Liberty groaned.

"It's a little funny," Liberty's mom said.

"It's a lot funny," SAM agreed.

"When I come to visit you in America someday, do I have to be perfect?" Nino asked her.

"Well, no," Liberty admitted.

"There! Now come, everybody is waiting for you!"
Nino said. Liberty allowed Nino to drag her back onto
the stage. The audience clapped.

"H-hi," Liberty stammered. She felt her face turn
red again. "Sorry about saying, 'I'm going to eat your
eyeballs.' I am not really going to do that."

The audience laughed.

"And sorry to everybody who is watching this on
live TV," Liberty said, addressing the TV camera.

"Oh, don't worry," the host called out. "This is not
live. We are taping it for later."

"Really?" Liberty perked up happily. "So you can
edit out the whole 'eating your eyeballs' part?"

"Do we have to?" the TV cameraperson called up.
"That's the best part! No, I'm just teasing. We won't
show that."

"Phew," Liberty said.

Everyone in the audience cheered. Liberty saw

that the people in the audience were smiling at her. Someone was waving a sign that said WE LIKE LIBERTY!

Liberty suddenly felt very, very happy.

"I am going to tell all my friends back home how awesome you are. And you can all come visit us anytime. Hey, you know what would be cool? A *supra* sleepover!"

Yeah, Liberty imagined a feast sleepover.

"Oh, the *supra* would make a great sleepover!" Liberty said. "You guys could all sleep over, I'll make great cookies. . . ."

Liberty's mother looked a little surprised. Liberty realized she was maybe getting carried away inviting hundreds of people to a sleepover.

"Okay, bye!" Liberty decided to quit while she was ahead.

"That was so nice," the host said, and took the microphone from Liberty's hands.

Mrs. Piffle came on and whispered to Liberty that there would be more grown-up speeches, so Liberty could go to the room offstage.

And then there was a noise.

Brrrrzzzzt.

Everyone looked around to see whose cell phone

was vibrating while the First Lady and First Daughter were onstage.

Brrrrzt.

Then Liberty realized whose cell phone was buzzing. It was the First Lady's! Her mother didn't realize it, though. She needed a rescue! Liberty walked over to her mom.

"Mom," she whispered, pointing at her mother's pocket.

Her mother looked like: Uh-oh.

Liberty reached in and plucked out the cell phone.

"Got you covered," she whispered. She took the phone and scurried off the stage.

Liberty went back to the waiting room. Nino was there.

"Hi, Liberty!" Nino said. "We can wait here while they do some more speeches. You were great."

"Thank you," Liberty said. "Thanks for helping me go back out onstage and—"

Brrrrzzzzt.

"Your pocket is buzzing," Nino pointed out.

"Oh, it's my mom's cell phone," Liberty said. "Usually she turns it off, but she forgot."

Liberty went to turn it off, but then saw what was making the noise.

"Oh, my mom's Skype is calling," Liberty said. "Hee. It's Mrs. Mellon."

Brrrrzzzzt.

Liberty thought about it. She wasn't allowed to have any chats on her cell phone. But her mom could! It would be cool to talk to someone overseas, even if it was just Mrs. Mellon. Liberty clicked on the answer button.

"Hello, Mrs. Mellon?" Liberty said. She saw the call get answered.

"How are you today? Guess what, Mrs. Mellon?" Liberty said. "I'm in the country of Georgia, which is halfway across the world from you!"

The video screen popped up. A close-up face filled the cell phone screen.

It was not Mrs. Mellon.

"Oh no," Liberty groaned. "Max Mellon, why are you Skyping my mom?"

"Hey, Liberty, is that you?" Max said. "I was just messing around with it to see if it works. I'm bored."

"Okay, well it works," Liberty said. "Hello and good-bye!"

"Liberty, are you chatting with a person from America?" Nino came over and peered at the cell phone.

"Yes," Liberty said. "On my mom's phone. But—"

"Oh, may I say hello to your friend?" Nino asked. "I'd love to talk to one of Liberty's friends in America."

She looked so eager it was hard to say no.

"Guess who I am?" Max was asking. He was pressing his nose back to look like a pig.

Oh no. Please don't say Piggerty Porter, First Snorter.

"It's—hey! Who's that?" Max spotted Nino.

"I'm Nino!" Nino said. "Do you like to pretend to be a pig? My cousin did that when he was a very little boy."

Max stopped acting like a pig. Heh.

"Nino, this is Max Mellon. Max, this is my nice friend Nino here in Georgia, another country, where I am representing the children of America."

Liberty hoped Max got the picture.

"Ha ha ha!" Max laughed. "Nino, has Liberty totally embarrassed herself yet?"

"No, not at all," Nino said.

Liberty looked at Nino. Then she looked at Max. And she suddenly decided to tell all.

"Actually, Max, Nino is being too nice. I did totally embarrass myself. In front of a huge audience of hundreds of people, and a television camera."

There.

At that moment, Liberty decided that she would never feel embarrassed again by Max. She had tried her best to be patriotical. She had tried her best to represent the children of America, and maybe she wasn't perfect, but she was the best First Daughter she could be.

"You did what?" Max was stunned.

"I meant to say something nice," Liberty said. "But instead I told them I was going to eat their eyeballs."

"You're kidding," Max said in disbelief.

"No, she is very serious." Nino nodded.

"I've got to tell everybody at school about that," Max said, and laughed.

"Go right ahead. It is pretty funny," Liberty admitted.

"I can't believe you told me that," Max said, shaking his head. "Respect."

He held his fist up to the camera. Liberty paused. Then she held up her hand and gave him a fist bump back.

"Aren't you going to call me Eat-Your-Eyeballs Porter?" Liberty asked. "Or Liberty Porter First Eyeballs?"

"Hah, those are good ones," Max said.

"Wait, what are you doing home? Aren't you supposed to be in school?" Liberty asked.

"I'm home sick," Max said. "I have a cold."

And that was when it happened.

Max Mellon's nose started to wiggle. He raised his right hand to itch his nose. And he sneezed. Not just a normal sneeze. A gooey, disgusting, gross *achoo*. And green sneeze flew out of his nose and onto the computer screen.

"Ewww, gross!" Liberty screamed.

"Eww, gross!" Nino screamed.

Max Mellon looked seriously embarrassed. And then it got worse for him.

"Max?" Max's mom's voice came over the phone. "Are you on my computer? You do not have permission to Skype—with the First Lady! Oh dear! Oh dear!"

Her face came onscreen.

"I'm sorry, oh dear," she said into the phone.

"Don't worry, Mrs. Mellon," Liberty said. "It's just me, Liberty. I have to go now. Bye."

Hee hee hee! That was excellent. Liberty and Nino laughed for about two minutes.

"You know what's weird? Here it's dinnertime, but at home they're in school," Liberty said. Speaking of school, she saw a familiar face on her mother's Skype list.

MR. SANTO

Her teacher! Liberty couldn't resist. She clicked on her teacher's face.

"What are you doing?" Nino asked her.

"Let's see if this works." Liberty smiled.

Boop, boop, booooooop!

"Hello? Mrs. Porter?"

It was Mr. Santo!

"Mr. Santo, it's me, Liberty!" Liberty said into the cell phone.

"Liberty?" Mr. Santo said.

"Are you in school right now?" Liberty asked.

"Why, yes," Mr. Santo replied. "I was rather surprised when I got a Skype from your mother on my phone, so I thought I'd better answer it."

"So wait, is the class there?" Liberty asked.

"Yes," Mr. Santo said.

"HI, CLASS!" Liberty shouted.

"Well, just a minute. This is unexpected, so please

give me a moment to gather the class. And also to hold the phone away from my ear," Mr. Santo said.

"Oops, sorry I shouted," Liberty said. "I'll be normal now."

"Why don't I call you back on the computer?" Mr. Santo said. "They'll see you better."

She heard Mr. Santo tell the class that they had a special Skype guest visitor. And then the connection was cut off.

Booop! Booop! Boop!

Liberty answered, and then suddenly, on her mom's phone:

LIBERTY'S CLASS!

Chapter 15

S HE PEERED CLOSER AT THE SCREEN. HER class was sitting on the reading rug! There was Quinn, waving at her. There was Preeta! There were Harlow, Kayden, and Emerson waving hi!

"Hi, everyone back in fourth grade in America!" Liberty was waving like a crazy person. "Hi, from the country of Georgia!"

"How's Georgia?" Mr. Santo asked.

"It's so great!" Liberty said. "This is how you say hi: *gamarjoba*. This is how you say thank you: *madlob*. Guess what? I got to stomp on grapes and go to a feast and dance like crazy, and my father did the robot and—" Liberty stopped talking as she saw everybody in her class cracking up.

"Well, that certainly sounds exciting," Mr. Santo said. "I hope you bring back pictures to show."

"Oh, there's someone I want you to meet!" Liberty said, and aimed the cell phone at Nino. "This is Nino, my new Georgian friend."

"Hi, Nino!" Liberty's class at home all waved to her.

"Hello," Nino said. "*Gamarjoba.* It is very nice to meet you on the computer. I have never met so many American children in my life."

Then Nino peered closely at the cell phone and looked puzzled. She waved, and then she put her thumbs against her temples and waggled her fingers.

Umm.

"Nino," Liberty whispered. "May I ask why you are doing that?"

"I'm saying hello to the boy," Nino explained, pointing to the computer screen. "That boy is saying a special American hello to me, yes?"

That was when Liberty saw it. Cheese Fries was putting his thumbs against his temples and waggling his fingers. Suddenly he dropped his hands.

"Cheese Fries!" Liberty yelled. Everyone in the class turned to look at him.

"Uh-oh," he said. "I'm busted. I thought only Liberty could see that."

Nino dropped her hands to her sides too.

"That was not a special American hello?" she said, looking embarrassed. But she wasn't the only one looking embarrassed.

"I'm sorry, Georgian girl," Cheese Fries called out.

"I didn't mean to embarrass you. I was just being silly. Ouch!"

Liberty saw his sister smack him on the shoulder.

"Wow, Nino," Liberty said. "That's a first. I've never heard Cheese Fries apologize for his behavior. You should feel very special, not embarrassed."

"Then I will," Nino said. "I will teach Cheese Fries our special hello in Georgian."

"Okay, cool," Cheese Fries said.

"First you put your arms like this." Nino hooked her hands under her armpits. "Then you move your arms like this."

Cheese Fries hooked his arms under his armpits. "This looks like a chicken flapping."

"Yes," Nino said. "There are many chickens in Georgia."

Cheese Fries flapped like a chicken.

Liberty, Nino, and James cracked up.

"American boy! I'm just being silly!" Nino said. "That was a joke!"

"Aw, man!" Cheese Fries said. "I totally fell for that. Good one."

The whole class laughed.

"Well, it's time for us to get back to math class," Mr. Santo said. "But it was very exciting to overseas chat with you all the way on the other side of the world. I usually only overseas chat with your mother about your homework when she's traveling. That reminds me. Did you do your math homework yet, Liberty?"

Umm.

"Can't hear you!" Liberty said. "Bad connection, gotta go."

She hung up quickly.

"Liberty," a voice came from behind her. It was her mother.

Oh, pickle.

"I'll do my math homework on the flight home on Air Force One, I promise," Liberty said before her mother could say anything else.

"Hmm," her mother said.

"I had to focus on important things like friendship with another country, Mom," Liberty said.

"I would discuss this further, but you've been asked to come out onstage again for the program," her mother said.

Mrs. Piffle ushered Liberty and her family to the stage again.

There was a crowd of people suddenly, and photographers and Secret Service agents.

"We have some very special guests," the host said.

The First Lady of Georgia was there! The FLOG! She came up onto the stage. She was very glamorous.

Everyone was cheering her on as she said hello to Liberty and everyone onstage.

Then the president of Georgia came onstage. Everyone was going crazy!

"Welcome to all," he said to the audience. "Please welcome our honored guest today."

Then the president of the United States walked onstage.

Liberty's dad was here! The audience went totally crazy. Liberty ran over to her dad and gave him a big hug.

"Hi, Daddy!" she said. Her dad kissed her on the top of the head and then waved to the audience.

Liberty's dad then talked to the crowd. He told them how wonderful the trip was. He talked about friendship between countries. He talked about . . .

Some other things Liberty sort of spaced out about. She was smiling at kids in the audience. Hello! Hello!

The POG started talking. And Liberty heard a word that got her attention.

"Gifts!" the POG said.

Ooooh! Gifts!

"President Porter and your wonderful family, as a thank-you for your kindness, we would like to give you gifts from the people of Georgia," the president of Georgia said.

He gave her parents cool gifts from his country.

"Liberty, I present a gift to you," he said.

It was a beautiful dark red dress.

"This is our national costume," he said. "You can wear it like the beautiful dancers of Georgia."

"I love it!" Liberty said. "I can pretend I'm at a *supra* at home and dance around in it!"

The First Lady gave her a doll that had a matching outfit. Liberty would put it in her room with her most special beanie pets.

"And we also have a gift for our special guest, James," the president of Georgia said.

"Excuse me?" James looked shocked. "As in me, James?"

"Come on, James!" Liberty said, urging him to come over.

Nino stepped up to James, carrying a blanket in her arms. She held it out to James. Liberty stood on her tiptoes to see what was inside it.

Inside was a . . . oh gosh!

A PUPPY!

It was a super-cute fuzz of white with light brown spots. The puppy lifted his big, wobbly head and peered out of the blanket.

"A puppy?" James gasped.

"A puppy?" pretty much everyone else gasped.

"We heard how much James liked our dogs here," POG said. "This one would like to live in America."

"It's one of Gogo's puppies!" Nino said. "He will grow up to look like Gogo."

"I—I—," James stammered. Nino handed him the puppy, and he stared at the dog, grinning. And then his face fell.

"I'm sorry, but I can't," James said. "My mother—"

"Your mother would like to graciously accept this gift." Mrs. Piffle came forward. "On behalf of my son, thank you, Mr. President."

No way! Liberty clapped her hands.

"I can have a dog?" James asked his mother in disbelief. "You said they're too messy. Plus they have terrible manners when they eat their food and greet people."

"That's what made me change my mind," Mrs. Piffle said. "Your manners are so wonderful now. There is no one at home for me to teach etiquette to. So instead, I will train the dog."

JAMES HAD A DOG!

"I'll name him Bruiser," James said happily.

"Oh my," Mrs. Piffle said.

Liberty couldn't believe James was going to have his very own dog! Franklin was going to have a new best friend! Then Liberty remembered what Gogo looked like.

"Mrs. Piffle," she said quietly. "You do know this dog is going to be hugenormous."

"Yes." Mrs. Piffle sighed. "As I told your friend Nino, we have a horse field behind our home. Bruiser will have plenty of room to roam."

Yay! Yay! The audience was oohing over the cute puppy. James held him up so everyone could see him on the big screens around the room.

She could not believe Mrs. Piffle had changed her mind about having a dog! Liberty saw her chance.

"Mom, isn't it awesome that Mrs. Piffle is letting James have a dog?" she asked her mother.

"Yes, it is," her mother said.

Liberty paused. Then she went for it.

"May I have a pony?"

"Sorry, but no," her mother said, and laughed. The audience laughed too.

Well, it was worth a try.

"Should I have gotten a horse as a gift as well?" the POG asked.

"NO!" Liberty's mother said. "I mean, thank you very much, but no."

"I love my costume," Liberty told him. She decided to show everyone how much she loved her costume.

She slid the dress on right over her clothes. The audience cheered. Liberty noticed that Mrs. Piffle looked especially pleased. Wearing a present must be nice manners.

"Dance, Liberty!" a child called out from the audience.

"Oh my gosh, I am so not a good dancer," Liberty protested.

"I saw you dance at the *supra* last night," the POG said.

"I'm not going to—I can't—I mean—," Liberty stammered, and then she had an idea.

"Wait, I will dance if everyone will dance with me," she announced. "Can we have some music?"

The band struck up a song. Nino was the first to dance. She raised her hands in the floaty Georgian way, and her feet started to move. And then everybody in the audience joined her.

"Dance party!" Liberty called out. She started dancing around the stage. James held up the puppy's paws and made his new dog dance.

The POG bowed to Liberty's mother, and they started to dance. Liberty's father held out a hand to the FLOG, and the two of them started to dance.

Liberty was happy to see he was not doing the robot. Even SAM was tapping his foot to the beat. It seemed like the whole world was dancing, and that was when Liberty thought of it.

She pulled her mother's cell phone out of her pocket and hit a button.

Boop, boop, boop.

"Hello? Mrs. Porter? Liberty?" Mr. Santo answered.

Liberty could barely hear him over the music.

"Mr. Santo! Fourth-grade class! We're having a dance party!" Liberty shouted into the cell phone. "Come dance with the people of Georgia!"

Liberty held up the cell phone so that Mr. Santo could see the audience dancing and hear the band playing. Mr. Santo looked confused for one second, then he got it.

"Dance party!" Liberty heard her classmates yell. They all jumped in front of the computer and started to dance.

That was when Liberty noticed that the cameraman in the audience had zoomed in on her cell phone. All over the giant screens around the ballroom, you could see Liberty's class dancing.

There was Quinn imitating Nino's Georgian style of dance. There was Preeta doing her Irish step dance. Sydney was doing the bump with Adam. Harlow,

Emerson, and Kayden were doing the dance they practiced on the playground.

Ha! Mr. Santo was doing the robot. Cheese Fries was doing . . . was doing . . . okay, Liberty had no idea what Cheese Fries was doing. But he was attempting to dance.

"Dance party in America!" the kids in the audience were saying as they watched the screens and danced along.

James was waving his puppy's paws in the air. Liberty danced over to him.

"I wish Franklin was here to dance with us too," she said.

"Give me one second," Mrs. Piffle said, and pulled out her own cell phone. "I know exactly where Franklin is. I was just talking to the White House."

Liberty didn't get it at first, until she saw Miss Crum's face on Mrs. Piffle's cell phone.

"Bertha?" Mrs. Piffle said.

Miss Crum's name was *Bertha*? Then Mrs. Piffle passed the cell phone to Liberty. Liberty saw Miss Crum sitting at her desk back in the White House and on her lap was . . .

FRANKLIN!

"Miss Crum!" Liberty said. "I didn't even know you liked Franklin!"

"Well," Miss Crum sniffed, "I was a bit lonely without all of you here at the White House. Franklin has been keeping me company."

"Yay!" Liberty said. "And now you both have to join our dance party."

James held Bruiser up to the cell phone screen, making his paws dance. Miss Crum lifted Franklin's paws and waggled them around too.

"Franklin's at our dance party." Liberty clapped her hands. "And you too, Miss Crum. Everybody's here."

And then she noticed something moving around on Miss Crum's shoulders.

"Suzy? Roosevelt?" Liberty gasped.

"The sugar gliders have been keeping me company too." Miss Crum shrugged. She patted Suzy on her left shoulder! And then Roosevelt snuggled up under her ear.

Yay, yay, and hurray! An international dance party—with pets!

Just then her father and mother twirled up to her. They were smiling.

"I think it has been a successful trip overseas," Liberty's father said. "And we couldn't have done it without you, First Daughter."

They couldn't have done it without her?

"First Daughter Fantabulous!" said Liberty. "First Daughter Friendtastic! And First Daughter Foreign-tacular!"

Many thanks to my:

CHIEF USHER: Fiona Simpson, chief editor

CHIEF *and* STAFF: Jon Anderson, Bethany Buck, Karin Paprocki, Alyson Heller, Carolyn Swerdloff, Venessa Williams, Paul Crichton, Katherine Devendorf, and Paige Pooler

SECRET SERVICE (LITERARY) AGENTS: Mel Berger, Lauren Heller Whitney, and Julie Colbert at William Morris Endeavor

FIRST HUSBAND: David DeVillers

FIRST DAUGHTER AND SON: Quinn and Jack DeVillers

FIRST DOG: Bradley Scruff DeVillers

LIBERTY PORTER, SUPER-SUPPORTERS: Mark McVeigh, Jennifer Roy, Robin Rozines, Amy Rozines, Melissa Wiechmann, Kent and Michelle Logsden, Julie Fisher, Jasmine Cameron, Laura Gehrenbeck, Veronika Shetelmakh, Masha Van Dreal, Kassie Culling, Tamara Abesadz, Prospero's Bookshop, QSI Tbilisi, and the U.S. Embassy of Georgia commissary for selling American snacks.